OLD BONES

OLD BONES

Lyn Jolley

CHIVERS

British Library Cataloguing in Publication Data available

This Large Print edition published by BBC Audiobooks Ltd, Bath, 2010.
Published by arrangement with the Author.

U.K. Hardcover ISBN 978 1 408 45734 4
U.K. Softcover ISBN 978 1 408 45735 1

Printed and bound in Great Britain by
CPI Antony Rowe, Chippenham and Eastbourne

2000

'Come on, Lizzie, we've arrived!' The wheels of the ambulance crunch to a halt on the gravel drive. 'You'll like it here, my love . . . like the Savoy this place is!' Elizabeth's wheelchair is carefully lowered to the ground. 'I think we'd better get your foot out of the way, Lizzie, or you'll be getting caught up.' The ambulance man lifts Elizabeth's foot on to the pram-like platform at the base of the chair in which she is transported, usually from bed to bathroom and back again. He hurts her knee; Elizabeth winces but her pain is not noticed. 'Right, up the wooden ramp, my love, and then I'll be getting back to the hospital. You'll soon be settled in—they're a good lot here.'

The ambulance man means to be kind, but Elizabeth is flustered by his enthusiastic efficiency. She is pushed quickly into a huge, old house, having no time to inspect its exterior.

A bell rings and a woman in a blue dress appears.

'Hello!' she says cheerily, smiling at Elizabeth with doubt behind her eyes.

'One Elizabeth Purley safely delivered,' the ambulance man announces, as though his patient were a parcel of china crockery.

'Jolly good!' replies the woman in blue. 'We'll soon have her all comfortable and cosy in her room.' And then, speaking in low tones to the delivery man, 'No trouble on the journey, was she?'

'No—no problems—poor old love,' he answers in similar voice. Then, 'Bye bye, Lizzie!' he calls and he is gone.

'Right—Lizzie, then, is it?' the woman deduces erroneously.

Her name is Elizabeth, and the fact that a stroke has left her unable to speak does not mean that she is deaf and senseless also.

Elizabeth is one hundred years old, born at the turn of the century, and, though her legs refuse to carry her and one arm lies heavy and numb by her side, her mind is agile, and frustrated by the non-cooperation of its ailing body.

The bell rings again. A young girl in a beige dress appears.

'Ah Jennifer!' the woman says. 'This is Lizzie, I'd like you to take her to her room and get her into bed if you would, please. She might need to go to the toilet—she's had a bit of a journey.'

The wheelchair moves smoothly along the corridor. Jennifer speaks to Elizabeth about the clement weather and its beneficial effect on the grounds, which surround the mansion. Elizabeth, however, in utter amazement, stares about her.

Is she losing her mind? No . . . she knows what she sees . . . and she knows this house. Some of it is altered. It is no longer a family home; it now houses the old who need somewhere to live until they die. To Elizabeth, though, it is so familiar. It should be . . . much of her life has been spent here.

The hallway is still panelled in rich, warming oak, and when they near its end, Jennifer steers Elizabeth's wheelchair into what was once the drawing room.

Doubts well in Elizabeth's mind. Is she mistaken? Can this tiny room really be part of her old, spacious home? Yes—yes it is! Between the rugs, which lay neatly on the floor, Elizabeth sees the dark, wooden boards, on which she slid in her stocking feet, more than once, as a child. And the door, against which her wheelchair now stands, is as it always was. The huge brass handle, which she had so often turned, is still there, gleaming, its ageless beauty unspoiled. In an instant of joy and forgetfulness, she tries to grab this shiny, tangible memory, but a motionless arm brings tears which sting her eyes.

Jennifer is busy preparing the bed. She does not notice Elizabeth's distress.

The old drawing room has been divided into little cells . . . no, she must not think in that way . . . Elizabeth rebukes herself; there are no iron bars. There is a bed, a single wardrobe and a chest of drawers.

Where once there was a family, there are strangers. Where once there was beauty and space, there is necessity and restriction.

'I'll just go and get your bag,' Jennifer says gently, 'we left it in the lobby. Then we'll pop you into bed, Elizabeth. Yes . . . I'm going to call you Elizabeth—it's such a lovely name, it's a pity to shorten it. I won't be a minute.'

It is uncomfortable in the wheelchair now. Elizabeth has been sitting for far too long and she will be glad to lie down.

Her eyes are drawn again to the brass door handle. She finds a strange solace in its familiarity . . . a familiarity which seems to blot out the years between then and now.

*   *   *

I remember when I could stand straight and look at my face in that golden mirror. It must have been when I was about six, and believed that everything that shone with a yellow glow was gold. I marvelled at the way in which the curves of the bulbous handle distorted my features, and I made faces at myself when no one was looking. I found great amusement in those grotesque reflections.

Once, when my brother Edward and myself were arguing, I pushed him hard and he fell and bumped his head on that door handle. He screamed, quite unnecessarily I felt. I ran and hid in the garden in case Nanny should be

4

angry with me. I was just a little frightened of Nanny.

*   *   *

'Right then, Elizabeth,' Jennifer says, as she returns with the old lady's bag and another young woman in a beige dress by her side, 'this is Denise. She's come to help me to get you into bed.'

Elizabeth's dressing gown is pulled gently from her. She is lifted onto the commode in the corner of the room.

'There we are, my lovely!' Denise enthuses, her strong Welsh accent filling the little room. 'Be a good girl for us.'

As she is lifted into bed, Elizabeth's eyes close and she sighs with relief. The aching muscles, which have held her back straight and her head up, loosen, and she feels drowsy. The bed is soft and the smooth, white sheets cool her where they touch her skin.

'I'll bring you some tea in a minute, Elizabeth,' Jennifer whispers.

'You'll finish off here then, will you, Jennifer?' the Welsh one sings.

*   *   *

Jennifer . . . Jenny . . . there was a Jenny then. I was about fifteen years old . . . yes . . . I remember the day she came to the house.

5

The first emotion I felt towards Jenny was jealousy. It was her hair—it was quite glorious. She had long, thick, silky tresses of the most vibrant, deep chestnut colour. When the sun shone on her, it seemed to pick out golden strands and others of the most vivid auburn. As her luxuriant hair hung down her back, it fell in soft, natural curls, which bounced gently as she walked. I would gladly have given all my wealth in exchange for her wonderful hair, because my own was fine and straight and the colour of dried mud. It had to be curled and waved and pinned up in order to look even remotely respectable. I hated that painful morning ritual and I pleaded with my maid, on many occasions, to let it be. My father, however, would not tolerate the resultant untidiness in his only daughter.

Jenny's face was too round to be beautiful. She had a pretty mouth, though, which turned up at the corners and afforded her a permanent smile. Her eyes were brown and, all too often, full of mischief.

It was Jenny who first made me look away from my family and outward to the world beyond this house.

It seems unbelievable now, but Jenny was the first person from the working class that I had ever really known—apart from Nanny, whose correctness and authority had always placed her in a class apart—as far as I was concerned anyway.

*　　*　　*

Plans for me to spend part of my adolescence in a Swiss finishing school were abandoned due to the outbreak of war. My father would not allow me to leave England during such dangerous times. Instead he persuaded my governess, Miss Treherne, to stay on and continue with the unrewarding task of attempting to educate me.

I was not a good pupil. No matter how I tried to concentrate on the wonders of whatever subject was at hand, my mind seemed quite ungovernable. It would lurch into daydreams and adventures of the strangest kind, usually involving journeys to faraway lands, which had fascinating names and were inhabited by swarthy but dashing Arabian types. This resulted in my knowledge of history, Latin and all the rest being very sparse. Though Miss Treherne usually reported to my father that I was making 'steady progress', I felt certain that he was aware of my shortcomings in the world of academia.

The only reason that I was not severely punished for my lack of attention in lessons was that I was female. My brother, Edward, who was three years my senior, was at that time about to leave his public school and go up to Oxford. He carried all my father's pride with him.

I knew quite early on that I was something of a disappointment to Father, when I heard him telling my mother that he was thankful I was a girl. He said that some unsuspecting male would have to take me on and keep me. Adding that he would make a list of all the suitable young men to whom I should be introduced at the appropriate time. He also admitted to Mother that he hoped they would not be too discerning in their choice of a wife, for if they were, I should never get anyone to marry me.

I remember wondering what would become of me if no one would 'take me on' . . . but I resolved not to worry about it . . . and I did not.

*   *   *

Jenny Todd was two years older than me. She had worked as a scullery maid and then a kitchen maid at a large house in London. When the family that employed her decided to go back to India, Jenny was taken on as a housemaid, by my mother.

Apart from her hair, the thing that struck me most about Jenny was her boldness. She was not like the other servants. When she came into the room, bringing a tea tray or whatever, she would look me straight in the eye, as though she were anticipating a word of

8

thanks. There was no rudeness in her, but she made it obvious from the directness, both in her expression and her manner, that she had expectations of her employers. And, though she was aware of her subservient position in the household, she somehow commanded a respect which others of her class merely hoped for.

Jenny held her head high as she went about her duties. She had a natural grace and composure which I envied.

In the warm weather, when my lessons were finished for the day, Jenny used to bring me my tea in the garden. There was no one else of my age in the house, now that Edward was up at Oxford, and I enjoyed talking to her. Of course, she could only stay for a few minutes before returning to her chores.

I was not sure why, but I wanted to learn as much as I could about Jenny Todd.

'Are you going out on your afternoon off, Jenny?' I asked one day.

'Not this week, Miss Elizabeth,' she replied. 'Why—is there something you wish me to do for you?'

'Well, only if you want to. It's just that we can never talk properly because you always have to hurry off . . . and I'd like to hear all about you.'

'About *me*? I'm not very interesting—you're sure to be disappointed.'

'Will you meet me . . . er . . . in the rose

garden? On Wednesday? That is your afternoon off, isn't it?'

'Yes, all right, Miss Elizabeth, I'll come at about half past three—when your lessons are finished.'

'Good—don't forget, will you?'

'Oh, I'll be there! I can't think why you want to know about me though.'

I felt excited. I wanted to make Jenny my friend. Had I known where that friendship was to lead, however, perhaps I would not have gone to the rose garden that Wednesday afternoon, but then again, perhaps I would.

*   *   *

It was a hot day at the end of June and the fragile fragrance of roses hung on the air. That part of the garden was surrounded by a high wall, to which thorny, rambling bushes clung, their blooms colourful and quite perfect.

'I've never been in here before,' Jenny said, as she gazed around her. 'It's lovely . . . and the scent!'

'Sit down next to me,' I urged, patting the rough, wooden bench.

She did.

'It seems very strange, being here with you, Miss Elizabeth.'

'Well it shouldn't!' I declared. 'Now, tell me all about yourself, Jenny.'

'But there's nothing much to tell!'

10

'Look, you know all about my family—you live here with us. I know nothing about yours. Tell me, where do you come from?'

'Well, I was born in Gossborough—you've probably heard of it, Miss Elizabeth.'

'Yes—yes, I have. It's a market town, isn't it?'

'That's right—it's about fifteen miles from here. There's a big army barracks there too. My family still live there—in the house where I was born. I didn't like living in London very much. I'm glad to be back near my home.'

'Have you any brothers or sisters?'

'Yes, I have two brothers. There's Jacky—he's ten now, and our Albert—he's just had his eighth birthday.' Jenny's bright eyes looked to the ground. She was suddenly sombre. 'It isn't easy for my mother—she's on her own now, you see. My Dad died nearly four years ago.'

'Oh dear . . . that must have been awful for you . . . for all of you.'

'It was all very sudden—he wasn't ill or anything like that. He used to work as a labourer for a builder, but now that he's gone, Mum has to take in washing.'

'She earns money by washing other people's clothes?' I remember the amazement I felt at the idea of such an occupation. Unfortunately, my expression must have shown the extent of my shock.

'There's nothing wrong with washing!' Jenny snapped indignantly. 'It's honest work—

11

and very necessary too!'

'Oh yes—I didn't mean . . .' I was floundering and very ashamed of myself. 'Jenny—please—I didn't mean that there was anything wrong with doing washing. I just didn't realize that you could earn enough money to live on in that way—that's all. Please don't be offended!'

Jenny was soon calm again, though her cheeks remained flushed.

'No, well you can't,' she explained. 'I give my mother most of what I earn here too, otherwise she'd never manage.'

'What a good thing she's got you!'

'It won't be long before our Jack can earn enough money to help. He delivers groceries for the corner shop on Saturdays already—that brings in a few extra pennies.'

'He'll have to leave school while he's still very young, I suppose.'

'He will, yes.'

'What do you think he'll do for a living?'

'Don't know—labouring I should think.'

'I see.'

Jenny and I talked for some time and throughout that evening her words lingered in my mind and troubled me greatly. As the servants waited on us during dinner—there being enough food on our table to satisfy several families in need—I wondered what Jenny's mother and her brothers were eating.

That night, I lay awake thinking, as I had

never done before because, that night, I thought about matters of importance. I realized, quite suddenly, what nonsense had filled my head until then.

I had always been aware that there was poverty, aware that only a few lived in the luxury which, to me, was the norm. My conversation with Jenny, however, had sparked my curiosity. To have to work to earn one's food, to live this week on what one had earned last week, to do absolutely everything for oneself—the whole idea of it intrigued me.

My father's family had occupied Maramar Grange, with its vast grounds, for over two hundred years. Ours was the largest estate for miles. I had never thought about money or where it came from. I had everything I wanted—and more—and, as is the case with most children, my thoughts reached out no further than my own needs and desires.

Now, though, now that I was no longer a child, I decided that I should become more knowledgeable about the way in which others lived.

When listening to Jenny, who spoke with such staunch pride about the difficulties her mother faced, I felt guilty. It was not so much a guilt born from the fact that I was wealthy and she was not, it was my ignorance about the plight of the less fortunate which caused me to search my soul.

Suddenly, my own life seemed to lack depth

. . . even meaning. It was as though I lived in a cocoon, where only the frivolous and affluent mattered. As a person, I was shallow and inadequate.

I resolved that, when I next spoke to Jenny, I would ask her to take me to her home for a visit. There was a compulsion within me to see for myself how the poor lived. I wanted to experience, if only for a short while, what they endured every day of their lives.

It was not that I pitied the working class; that would have been patronizing and insensitive. No, I felt fascinated by their strength and their independence—I was in awe of them. I decided that I would get as close to these people as they would allow.

Jenny was surprised when I asked her if I could visit her home. She agreed, however, after some hesitation and much bewilderment, that we could go to Gossborough on her next afternoon off.

We had to devise a tale to tell my parents because they would never have approved of such an outing. So, I told my mother that I wanted to go shopping on my own—meaning without her or Miss Treherne—for the first time. I said that I realized she would not allow me to go entirely unaccompanied, so I suggested that Jenny should come with me. Mother was apprehensive and was only persuaded not to ask Father's opinion by my insistence that Jenny Todd was extremely

14

sensible, being two years my senior, and that we should be home by six o'clock.

I had never been on a train before. I told Mother that part of my treat would be to travel by steam engine. The chauffeur, therefore, was not troubled on this occasion and our true destination remained a secret.

*   *   *

The village station was not far from the boundaries of our estate. As Jenny and I walked down the lane, I took her arm. She seemed at ease with me and I was elated because I felt that we were truly becoming friends.

We sat in a compartment of our own. As the train carried us to Gossborough, we talked and laughed as two sisters might have done. Blakiston, the butler, was the main butt of our girlish jokes. He was so utterly pompous that he invited such derision from all who came into contact with him. Jenny and I, after much discussion, decided that neither of us had ever seen him smile. So, we made a promise that the first one to observe this unlikely phenomenon would search out the other, be it night or day, and give full details of what had provoked such an event.

After what seemed like a very short journey, the train pulled into Gossborough Station. The day was hot and airless as we alighted

15

onto the platform. Jenny explained that it was market day and so the town would be busier than usual. The train from London had just arrived on the other platform. As its occupants spilled out and jostled for space, the station became crowded. I had never before been in such close proximity to so many noisy strangers. I was somewhat alarmed and held on to Jenny's arm. As we made our way to the street, I looked back at the bustling scene and savoured the metallic smell of the trains in that steamy atmosphere. It was a relief, though, to be outside again.

Gossborough was alive with activity. We soon came to the market square, where stall-holders shouted the price of their goods in rough, roguish voices, whilst animals, imprisoned in untidy pens, lazed in the heat awaiting their fate.

Jenny led the way across the square and into one of the narrow, cobbled streets which joined it.

The terraced houses were tiny, with front doors that opened straight out onto the pavement. I was struck by their sameness. They reminded me of a row of shabby doll's houses.

'I live along here,' Jenny said. 'This is Prince's Lane, not that you'd ever find a prince within a hundred miles of it!'

The street was much quieter than the market place had been. I remember seeing a horse and carriage clattering along the cobbles. It stuck in my mind because it had to stop at the end of the lane where a motor car was crossing its path. The driver of the car shouted angrily at the man in the carriage to wait and let him pass. It made me think of how the old must always give way to the new, and, for a moment, I was saddened because the new seemed cold and unfriendly.

'What number is your house, Jenny?' I asked, feeling more than ready for refreshment.

'Number fifty—here we are!'

I suddenly felt nervous.

Jenny took a key from her purse and unlocked the front door. Once inside the house, we stood in a tiny passage. It was dark, after the brightness of the day, and cool too.

'I expect Mum's in the back kitchen,' Jenny said, showing me along the hallway.

The house smelled of cabbage and there was a staleness in the air which made me want to open all the windows.

'Ah, Jenny!' exclaimed the woman standing at the sink. 'How are you, my lovely?'

They kissed and hugged each other with an enthusiasm and warmth which was quite unlike the more restrained and proper embraces that I was used to.

'I'm fine, Mum—and I've brought a visitor.'

'Yes, so I see!' Jenny's mother looked troubled. 'You might have told me you were bringing a friend, Jenny—I'd have straightened the place up a bit.' The woman turned to me and shook my hand as though we were old friends. 'So, you work at the Purley's house too, do you, love?' she asked.

'Er . . . well . . .' I mumbled, turning to Jenny for guidance.

'Mum,' she interrupted, seeing my anxiety, 'this is Miss Elizabeth Purley.'

Jenny's mother snatched her hands away from mine. She stepped back from me, as though I were infected with some terrible disease, and made a kind of curtsey.

'Oh, Jenny!' she gasped, her eyes wide with disbelief. 'How could you? I . . . I'm so sorry, Miss Purley. I don't know what to say, really, I don't. Please, come into the front room—it's a little tidier in there. If I'd known you were coming, Miss, I'd have had a good clean through. We're in a bit of a mess, I'm afraid . . . it's my boys . . . they leave a pickle everywhere they go!'

'Please, Mrs. Todd,' I said, trying to placate the poor woman, 'I am perfectly happy to sit in your kitchen, and please, call me Elizabeth.'

'Oh well . . .' she whispered with some hesitation, 'I don't know if I should . . . it doesn't seem right . . . not right at all.'

'I am Jenny's friend, Mrs. Todd,' I insisted, 'and I want you to call me Elizabeth—please.'

'Oh, all right then—if you say so. It'll seem very odd though.'

18

She looked awkward and inept in her own kitchen and I felt unhappy because it was my presence that made her so.

'I'll make us some tea,' Jenny put in, obviously trying to lessen the tension.

'And me with no biscuits or cake in the house!' Mrs. Todd declared with shame in her tone.

'A cup of tea is all I want—really.' I tried desperately to be reassuring.

Mrs. Todd tidied hurriedly around me as I sat at the food-stained, wooden table in the middle of the cramped kitchen. Jenny poured the tea.

'I can't think why a young lady like you would want to visit us,' Mrs. Todd exclaimed. 'I don't mean that you're not welcome, of course, Miss P . . . Elizabeth. No, it's a real honour to have you here.'

'I told you, Mrs. Todd,' I replied gently, 'I'm Jenny's friend, so I wanted to meet you.'

The woman was clearly incredulous.

'Yes, I see,' she murmured shyly.

'I suppose your sons are both at school?'

'Yes, they'll be home before too long though—and then there'll be no peace!'

'I'm looking forward to meeting them. I have a brother, Edward, but he's three years older than me.'

There was a short pause, during which we sipped our tea and Mrs. Todd fidgeted nervously.

'I was telling Miss Elizabeth that it isn't easy for you, now that Dad's gone,' Jenny began, considering it preferable to talk of something melancholy than not to talk at all.

'Oh, everyone's in the same boat now that the men have gone to war,' her mother answered, making light of her difficulties. 'I'm managing quite well, and don't you go telling people any different, Jenny.'

I saw a fierce pride in Mrs. Todd, just as I had seen in her daughter. There were few other obvious similarities between them. Jenny's mother was thin and her features were pointed. Only the colour of the eyes and hair were the same. I decided that Jenny must resemble her late father.

Gradually, as we talked of the war and its effect on us all, the tensions between us subsided. I must admit, though, that I was somewhat ashamed to confess that my main grievance about the hostilities was that I was unable to travel to Switzerland and finish my education there. When I thought of what others were suffering, I wished that I had kept that slight inconvenience to myself.

As we chatted, I glanced around the little room. Apart from the table and chairs, at which we sat, the kitchen equipment comprised only of a small stove in one corner and some shelves by the sink, which hosted the family's pots and pans. There was a door, slightly ajar, which led to the scullery. Through this, I could see the copper, which Mrs. Todd must have used for all the washing, though at the time, I had no idea what such an ugly object could be.

After a while, the two boys came rushing in through the back door. They hugged Jenny with great excitement and stood with curiosity on their grubby faces, and caps in their even grubbier hands, as they were introduced to me.

Jacky and Albert were very much alike. Their round faces and smiling eyes ensured that both bore a strong similarity to their elder sister.

Mrs. Todd produced bread and cheese for the boys whilst they told us, with much satisfaction, about the school bully, who had been chastised in front of the whole class, much to the delight of the rest of the long-suffering pupils.

Jenny and I were offered bread and strawberry jam. I felt that I should accept, in case Mrs. Todd thought my refusal to be ill mannered or, even worse, a veiled gesture against her simple hospitality. The bread was thick and dry, but I ate it with feigned enthusiasm and remarked on the tanginess of the jam.

At half past four, we left Jenny's house so that we might catch the train and get back to Maramar Grange before six o'clock, as promised.

Mrs. Todd was very kind. She assured me

that I would be welcome in her home whenever I felt inclined to visit. Though she tried manfully to conceal her true feelings, her sense of relief at my departure, however, was obvious. I thanked her for her hospitality and we left her, waving from the front door step. It was still very hot and we were not inclined to hurry.

The traders in the market square were packing up their goods and laden shoppers were making their way home.

Suddenly, raised voices could be heard from among the empty stalls. They were not cheerful, cajoling voices, as they had been before, but harsh, contentious shouts. I craned my neck and stood on tiptoes to see what was happening. The argument appeared to be about money.

Jenny slipped her arm through mine and pushed me gently forward. We were compelled to stop immediately, though, as a man went sprawling across the cobbles right in front of us. He groaned and shook his head before stumbling to his feet. Another, larger man emerged from between the stalls. The two of them stared at each other, their faces wild with hatred.

I stood, transfixed, as the men began to punch each other. They were vicious—like two dogs fighting over territory. I had never before seen human beings behave in such a way. The shock caused me to feel nauseous.

The men's clenched fists flew savagely in all directions. Some blows reached their intended target, whilst others connected with nothing but the air.

By now, there were several onlookers, some of whom shouted encouragement at one or other of the disputants . . . evidently taking some pleasure from this horrifying spectacle.

Suddenly, the smaller of the two men lurched towards me. Blood was splattered all over my skirt, as a huge split in the skin above his eye gushed alarmingly. He staggered before me, blinded by his own blood, which mingled with the dust as it fell, like thick, red paint, onto the cobbled street.

My legs began to tremble. I felt dizzy and faint. The muscles round my stomach seemed to harden and form themselves into painful knots. Staring at this man, with his face gashed open and his blood pouring all over him, I knew true fear for the first time in my life. I felt vulnerable and so exposed to the real world that my instinct was to run as fast as I could and find somewhere to hide.

Just as I thought that the strength in my legs was about to desert me altogether, two policemen ran past me and grabbed at the tiring fighters. The crowd jeered, as the offenders were dragged roughly away, the wounded man protesting his innocence and demanding that justice be done.

The onlookers dispersed quickly, and only

the man's blood remained as evidence that a brawl had taken place.

'Oh, Jenny, how awful!' I gasped, my heart still racing.

'I know. There's a fight nearly every market day. I just hope it hasn't made us late for the train!'

Jenny's acceptance of what we had just witnessed was as much of a shock to me as the fight itself had been. The difference between our backgrounds and our experience of life had never seemed so enormous, but, at this moment in time, I wanted to deny that such differences existed, so I did.

I trembled as we walked to the station and only the realization that we had, in fact, missed the train, caused me to put the fight to the back of my mind.

A different anxiety took control of me . . . a more familiar one . . . the anxiety which gripped my insides whenever I thought that I might have incurred my father's wrath.

*   *   *

We had to wait over an hour for the next train, and it was after seven when we arrived back at Maramar Grange.

I can see Miss Treherne now, an air of urgency competing with the foreboding, as she stood just outside this drawing room door and greeted Jenny and myself with the news that

Father wished to see us both in his study . . . immediately.

'Don't worry,' I whispered to Jenny, with unconvincing confidence, 'I'll take the blame.'

'If I get the sack . . . what will my mum do?' Jenny was holding back the tears, but only just.

'I won't let him sack you!' My brave words and adamant tone belied totally the panic which I felt.

My father stood in front of his desk, his huge frame overshadowing us and adding an aura of superiority and strength to his authority.

He was nearly twenty years older than my mother, but his hair was still dark, and his face, with its broad forehead and well defined eyes, was still handsome.

His expression was intimidating and his stance threatening.

'It wasn't Jenny's fault at all, Father!' I blurted out, in earnest desperation. 'It was me! I made her take me shopping and it was my dawdling that caused us to miss the train. She kept telling me to hurry . . . it was all my fault!'

When I stopped to draw breath, I noticed that my father's eyes had fixed on my skirt—I had forgotten the blood! He stooped in order to inspect the stains more closely.

'How did you get blood on your clothing, Elizabeth?' he asked slowly and quietly.

I hesitated, my mind trying frantically to produce a feasible excuse.

25

'Tell the truth,' Jenny urged.

'That's good advice, Elizabeth,' Father added.

My heart was leaden. I knew that he would be angered by the truth.

'We saw a fight, Father,' I admitted.

'Where did you see a fight?'

There was an alarming calmness in my father's voice. It was as though he were holding all his fury in check until the appropriate moment, when he would release it like a gun releases a bullet—with lethal force and terrible consequences.

'It was in the market square—in Gossborough.' I returned his stare with my reply, determined that he should not consider me to be intimidated.

'Gossborough?'

'Yes . . . I visited Jenny's home.'

My father looked at my friend.

'Your name is . . . Jenny . . . ?'

'Jenny Todd, Sir.'

'Why did you take my daughter to visit your home, Jenny Todd?'

Father's arrogance, when he spoke to Jenny, infuriated me.

'Because I asked her to!' I put in before she could summon an answer. 'You are not to blame Jenny, for any of this . . . it was all my idea!'

Father looked at us both in turn. He folded his arms, as if the action would aid in his assessment of the situation.

'Go back to your duties, Jenny Todd,' he ordered. Jenny did not argue. 'Now then, Elizabeth,' he went on, turning to me, 'I think you owe me an explanation, don't you?'

'I'm sorry I was late, Father,' I replied, relieved that Jenny had been allowed to go, 'but the fight in the market square was right in front of us, and by the time the police had taken the men away, our train had gone.'

'You told your mother that you were going shopping in town, not on a fifteen-mile trip to Gossborough! You lied, Elizabeth!'

His voice was louder now and more accusing.

'I'm sorry I lied, but if I had told you or Mother that I wanted to visit Jenny's family in Gossborough, you would have stopped me going.'

'Well, you've managed to get that right at least,' he said sarcastically. 'Of course we would not have agreed to such an outing!'

'But why—just because Jenny is a servant?'

'Yes—that's exactly why!'

'She's my friend!'

'Don't be ridiculous, Elizabeth! You can't understand what friendship is, if you believe that you can ignore the difference in your class and hers!'

My indignation was gaining momentum, just as my father's was.

'You mean that because she is poor and we

are rich, I can't be her friend?!'

'It isn't just a matter of money!'

'Oh no, I suppose breeding and birthright must come into it too!'

I had never before argued with my father—not many people did—but I was suddenly enjoying my newly found boldness.

'Elizabeth! I would remind you of your manners!'

'I am no longer a child, Father, and I cannot simply accept what you say anymore without questioning the logic behind your words.'

I was trying to appear dignified, hoping that an air of maturity might add weight to my argument.

'How dare you!'

'I dare, Father, because I see no reason why Jenny and myself cannot be friends.'

He was taken aback by my continuing defiance.

'Elizabeth!'

'I went to her home. I met her mother and her younger brothers—her father is dead. They are good, honest people, and I don't care which class they belong to—I want to be a friend to them!'

'You are showing your naivete, Elizabeth! I dare say that Jenny . . . Jenny . . . what's her name?'

'Todd—Jenny Todd!'

'Yes . . . I dare say that she is honest. She wouldn't be employed here if she were not.

But that doesn't mean that you can ignore all the standards which a young woman in your position is expected to uphold!'

'My position! Just because I was born in this house and not in Prince's Lane, Gossborough! Can't you see, Father, that Jenny and I are both young women! We enjoy each other's company—we like to talk—so, what does it matter where we were born or who our parents are?'

'It matters far more than you realize—that's obvious!'

'You think that people like Jenny are inferior to us, don't you?'

My father was unaccustomed to being questioned in such a way. He tried to avoid answering me by intensifying his own anger.

'You will have no more to do with that girl!' he shouted. 'And that is the end of the matter!'

'They are not in any way inferior!' I continued, refusing to be silenced. 'I'll tell you something, Father . . . I feel privileged to have met Mrs. Todd and Jenny . . . do you hear me? Privileged! There is a kind of splendour in their way of life! And there are millions more like them, who struggle courageously on from day to day barely managing to feed their children. I'm just beginning to realize what a spoilt brat I've been and I want to change— I'm going to change!'

'Elizabeth, be quiet!'

'We should be in awe of such people,

Father, instead of looking down our over privileged noses at them!'

'And what if I dismiss Jenny Todd?' he said smugly. 'Then her family's income would be severely cut. And, if I refuse to give her a reference, she won't find another job in the area!'

'You wouldn't be so cruel!'

'I haven't decided what to do yet.'

'Please don't sack her, Father!' I pleaded.

'Ah!' he smirked. I hated him when he did that. 'So . . . who depends on whom? Where would the likes of Jenny Todd be without us?'

'That's only power!'

'ONLY power?'

'Yes—and you haven't earned it—you were merely born to it!'

'MERELY?' My father's fury surged.

'It seems to me, that the fact that people like you should have any hold at all over people like the Todds, only shows how foolish and unjust our society is!'

I knew I had gone too far, but to have said what I really felt was enormously satisfying.

'That's enough!'

Father took hold of my arm. I struggled, but he pulled me to the door.

'What are you going to do to Jenny?' I cried.

'Go to your room!' he roared, no longer able to accept the rebellious words of his only daughter. 'You will have no more to do with that girl! It must be her influence that is affecting you and filling your silly head with such arrant nonsense! I shall see that she is only allowed to work below stairs from now on! If you disobey me, Elizabeth, I shall dismiss her! Now go!'

I ran to my room crying aloud, but my tears sprang from anger and frustration—not fear.

*   *   *

'Wakey wakey, Lizzie!' The Welsh voice is back again. 'You are a dreamy one. Come on now, here's a lovely boiled egg for your breakfast. Let's have you sitting up.'

The food is tasteless and the tea only warm.

Elizabeth does not want to be washed and sat in the wheelchair. She likes to be in bed. Warm hands lift her, however, convinced that they know best. They clean her and comb her fine, white hair.

'It's a sunny day, Lizzie. You could sit out on the balcony for a while.' The Welsh voice sings on. 'We'll put a blanket round your legs. There we are—nice and warm—off we go!'

Elizabeth is pushed out of her little room and along the hallway. The wheelchair is turned to the right, and suddenly she sees the grand staircase, wide and curved, in front of her.

*   *   *

My heart was pounding in my chest, like a rhythmic jungle drum, as I ran up that elegant staircase in the middle of the night, all those years ago.

Everywhere there was darkness, like a black, protective screen. It concealed my illicit movements. All the occupants of Maramar Grange had been sleeping for some time . . . all except me. I had been determined not to sleep. Lying there, waiting for the right moment, I had felt excited, like a child longing for Santa Claus to come, but, at the same time, frightened of his mysterious presence.

Once I was on my feet, however, and out of the safety of my bedroom, I grew intensely aware of the fact that to be discovered would mean dire punishment.

My feet were bare, and I held up my nightclothes away from them in case I should trip.

Firstly, I crept downstairs to make absolutely certain that the light in Father's study was out. It was, and so was the one in the drawing room . . . he was in bed.

I ran up the main staircase, which I knew so well. I was sure-footed and hardly out of breath. Once at the top, I tiptoed past Father's room and Mother's, then Edward's and then my own. I carried on to the end of the hallway and opened the door, which led up to the next floor. This staircase was narrower. I held tightly on to the handrail because this way was not so familiar to me. I reached the top. Nanny's room was on this floor, so were Blakiston's and Cook's and poor Miss Treherne's—my patient and long-suffering governess. My business, however, was with none of these.

In the darkness, I could just make out the door, behind which was the other staircase. This was the one used by the servants to go from the kitchens, below stairs, to their rooms at the very top of the house. Through this door, up one more flight of stairs and I would come to the attic rooms.

I had never had occasion to go this way, and my muscles tensed with every board that creaked under my feet. The total blackness was becoming claustrophobic. This final staircase was so narrow that I touched the walls on either side of me as I ascended. My breathing was rapid now, both from the effort of climbing so many stairs and from the anxiety of not knowing exactly where I was. My foot searched for another stair—no—I must be at the top.

I remember laying the palms of my hands flat on the cold walls so that I could feel along the passage for the doors of the attic rooms. Jenny's was the third one along—she had told me so. I wondered if it would be locked. I was afraid that she would scream out in fright when I tried to enter.

Gently I tapped on the door and pushed it

open.

'Jenny . . . it's me . . . Elizabeth,' I whispered, closing the door behind me.

'Miss Elizabeth!'

I heard bedclothes being thrown back, a sound which I would not have noticed had I been able to see. The lamp was lit and, as the world became visible again, I thought that if I ever went blind I should probably take my own life, because a blackness which never ended would be unbearable.

'Oh, Jenny!' I hugged my friend.

'You shouldn't be up here, Miss Elizabeth!' she implored. 'What would happen if your father found out?'

'Oh he's asleep—don't worry—I made sure of that! I just had to see you, Jenny, after that awful business the other day. Mother assured me that Father wouldn't sack you, but I had to be certain that you were all right.'

'Yes, of course I am. I'm confined to the kitchens, that's all—it doesn't bother me.'

'I'm so sorry, Jenny. The last thing I wanted to do was get you into trouble.'

'Don't worry about it—I've still got a job— that's the main thing.'

'But it's all so unjust!'

'We were very late, Miss Elizabeth—and we did lie about where we were going.'

'No—I don't mean that, Jenny. I mean . . . your life and mine . . . being so different. It's so unfair. It makes me angry! Doesn't it make

34

you feel angry?'

'It's just the way things are. If I get all worked up about it, nothing will change—so what's the point?'

'But you shouldn't just accept it like that!'

'I can't do much else!'

'No . . . I suppose not. But you don't feel inferior, do you? Promise me that you'll never feel inferior to anyone!'

'I know that I am a servant, Miss Elizabeth, and I probably always will be, but I have never considered myself to be a lesser person because of it.'

'No, I thought not—you have such a proud face. Don't let anything ever change that opinion, Jenny—not anything or anyone.'

*   *   *

After that night, I visited Jenny every week. We talked about our families, and she told me of her neighbours in Prince's Lane, whose men were at war, and of the young soldier she had met near the Gossborough Barracks.

'He's got to go to France soon, Elizabeth,' she explained to me one night . . . I had finally persuaded her to drop the 'Miss'. 'All they seem to do at the barracks now is kit them out, teach them to use a rifle and bayonet . . . and then they're off to the front.'

'You're very fond of him, aren't you?' I asked, knowing full well what the reply would be, by the look in Jenny's eyes whenever she spoke of her Stanley.

'Yes, I am, and I wish he didn't have to go and fight.'

'He'll be all right, Jenny,' I said reassuringly, though I was painfully aware that my words of comfort meant very little.

'Perhaps, when he conies home on leave, you could meet him, Elizabeth.'

'I'd like that!' I enthused. 'It would be marvellous to talk to someone who has actually been to war.'

The next time I visited Jenny, she told me that Stanley had gone to France. She cried, and asked me to pray with her for the safety of all the soldiers. I felt hypocritical as I prayed because, for some time, I had doubted the existence of a God.

*   *   *

'Has she ever been married?' Denise asks the woman in the blue dress, as they look out of the French windows to where Elizabeth sits in her wheelchair.

'No, apparently not. It says Miss Purley on the admission form.'

'She's wearing a wedding ring but it's on the wrong finger.' Denise's Welsh voice sings in whispered tones.

The woman in the blue dress and Denise think that Elizabeth is asleep, but the French windows are open, and she listens, with her eyes closed, to what they say.

'It's probably her mother's ring.'

'I'll bet it's worth a bit. They don't make them of such thick gold nowadays. Has she got any family at all?'

'There's no next of kin on the form, so I suppose she's on her own . . . poor old love.'

The sun shines on Elizabeth's gold ring.

*   *   *

It was the summer of 1917 before I finally met Stanley. By this time he and Jenny had decided that they would marry when the war was over.

My dear mother had died in the warm, embryo summer of 1916, and Father's grief had so engulfed him that his stern control over my movements had slackened somewhat. He seemed to have resigned himself to the fact that a seventeen year old daughter could no longer be confined to her home. Miss Treherne had left just after my mother's death, and, to my surprise, Father seemed in no hurry to employ anyone else. Neither was it necessary for Jenny and myself to go on meeting at night, because Father had ceased to restrict her to duties below stairs. He was either unaware of our continuing friendship, or he no longer cared about it.

For the first time in my life I felt sorry for Father. He was aimless and his great strength, which I had so often loathed, seemed to have left him. Most of his days were spent alone in his study, and the barriers between the two of us were too great for me to bring him solace. So, with my brother Edward up at Oxford, Father and myself each mourned alone and in our own way.

I do not know how I would have coped without Jenny during those first months after my mother's death. She was closer to me than a sister could have been.

'Stanley's coming home on leave next week!' she announced one bright morning at the beginning of June. 'Come to Gossborough with me on my afternoon off and meet him. I know you'll like him.'

It was a relief to get away from Maramar Grange. I had not been back to Gossborough since Jenny and I had seen the fight in the market place. The resulting altercation with Father seemed an age ago, as we arrived once again at Gossborough Station.

We were to meet Stanley in a teashop near the Market Square.

'There he is!' Jenny squealed with pride. 'He is waiting outside for us.'

I was introduced to a tall, slim young man whose face was not handsome, but amiable and honest. Yes, I thought that Stanley would do very well for my friend. He ushered us into the teashop, where another soldier sat at a table apparently awaiting our arrival.

'This is David,' Stanley announced. 'He's been injured . . . shot in the shoulder, so he's back home till he's completely fit again.'

We all shook hands, then tea and cakes were ordered. Stanley talked about the fighting he had seen and the dreadful conditions in which the soldiers lived. Though I was horrified as I listened to him, I felt certain that he was concealing the worst of it to protect Jenny and myself from too much stark reality.

After our refreshments, the four of us walked to the edge of town where the barracks stood, grey and austere. Behind the huge building lay the woods, which skirted Gossborough. The four of us strolled, in the heat of the afternoon, towards the shade of the trees. Jenny took Stanley's arm whilst I walked with David.

He told me how he had been wounded. His shoulder was evidently still very painful, but he made light of it.

David was shy. He spoke quietly and rarely looked me in the face. When he did, though, there was an innocence in his large, steel-grey eyes, which was somehow disarming. His hair was fair and wavy, and his features classical and in proportion, but it was those wonderful eyes that dominated his suntanned face.

The afternoon passed quickly and, at five o'clock, the boys saw us to the train.

'Well—what do you think?' Jenny asked, her

39

eyes alight with anticipation.

'I think that Stanley is a splendid chap,' I replied, 'you've made the right choice there, Jenny.'

'He's grand, isn't he?'

'Yes, he certainly is. Let's just hope that this awful war will be over soon, so that you can be married. I will get an invitation to the wedding, won't I?'

'Of course you will!' Jenny smiled knowingly. 'David's a handsome lad, don't you think?' she added.

'Yes, yes . . . he's very nice . . . I like him a lot.'

We said nothing more about David that day. When I went to bed that night, however, his gentle voice was all I could hear and, when I closed my eyes, his face was there before me.

* * *

During that leave of Stanley's, the four of us met often, usually in the densely wooded countryside which surrounded Maramar Grange.

It was a warm, sunny June. We went for long walks and talked for hours, about everything imaginable.

I felt happy for the first time since my mother's death. I hardly noticed my brother Edward's presence when he returned home for the summer vacation, except that he kept

40

Father occupied—which was all to the good.

After Stanley's return to France, David and I continued to meet. I began to dread the day that his shoulder was healed. I wanted him with me—not on some French battlefield.

*   *   *

I think it was his calm, compassionate manner which first attracted me to David. He was so utterly different from my authoritarian father.

His young life had been spent with his grandmother in a Derbyshire village. He was a true countryman. It fascinated me to hear him identify a species of bird by its song, or to watch as he searched out squirrels and rabbits for my delight.

David was a young man who enjoyed the simplicity of nature. He loved the quiet of the countryside and the life out of doors. His views were uncomplicated, and I found him refreshing to be with.

I remember one day, when he picked up a fledgling that had fallen from its nest. Though his strong hands had been used to hard work, I was mesmerized by the tenderness with which he lifted the tiny, fragile bird, and returned it to its mother. He had great respect for all forms of life, and no desire to have power or control over any creature.

A more unlikely man to go to war, I could not imagine. I wondered how he could possibly cope with the barbarity of the battlefield. The very idea of David trying to kill or maim another human being was absurd and quite obscene.

I never broached the subject of war. It seemed to me that he wanted to forget, as far as he could, that he would have to return to France and the fighting. On one occasion, though, David himself brought up the subject, and he would not be silenced.

'Going to war didn't bother me much until now,' he confided, as we walked through the lush grass of a spacious glade in Maramar Woods. It was just after Stanley had gone back to France, and we were both feeling low.

'Don't talk about it, David,' I pleaded, 'you won't have to go back for ages yet.'

'No, there's something I want to explain, Elizabeth. Something I must explain. I told you before how my parents both died when I was young . . .'

'Yes, you did.'

'Well, once my grandmother had passed away, there was no one who really mattered to me. I had friends, of course, but they were all going off to war, so it seemed the natural thing for me to go too. When the others used to get letters from home, I realized just how alone I was. I envied them—there was nobody to care whether I survived the trenches or not.'

'It'll never be like that again. David.'

We sat down on an old tree stump. The

thick foliage of the oaks sheltered us from the sun's glaring and pitiless rays.

'I'm not a good soldier, Elizabeth.'

David's eyes were sorrowful, and I felt that I wanted to protect him from any more sadness.

'You're not saying that just because you were shot, are you?'

'Partly, I suppose.'

'Well then you're being silly, David. Hundreds of soldiers are wounded every day. It doesn't mean that they're not good at their job—it's simply bad luck.'

'You don't understand. I wanted to get to France, but more to be with my mates than anything else. There was nothing for me here. It wasn't until I actually got there, that I realized just what was involved in being a soldier at the front.'

'I'm sure you're not the only one who felt like that.'

'It's typical of me, Elizabeth. My gran always used to say that I should think ahead. She said that my biggest fault was rushing into things without considering the consequences. I was so keen to volunteer and, at the beginning, the camaraderie was good for me . . . I felt part of it all. The first time I saw action, though, I wanted to run away.'

'David . . . you mustn't worry if you felt scared . . . that's natural. All the others must have felt exactly the same . . . if they're honest about it.'

43

'I know it's normal to feel frightened, but the others don't let that fear affect their actions ... I did.'

'What do you mean?'

'I couldn't fight, Elizabeth. I froze. When I saw young men falling all round me—from both the English and the German lines—I was so absolutely petrified that I couldn't move. That's how I got this.' David looked down at his shoulder. He sneered. 'If that wound had been a couple of inches to the right, I'd have been a dead man. Yet, when I felt the pain and saw the blood, I was relieved. I knew that I'd be out of the fighting. You see ... I'm nothing more than a coward. I had to tell you the truth.'

'It just so happens, David, that I don't consider a reluctance to kill others to be cowardly. You're a very sensitive person, and you were shocked by your first experience in battle—that's very understandable.'

David shook his head.

'What will happen next time?' he murmured.

'Oh, David ... you must defend yourself!'

'Perhaps, now that you're here, waiting for me, I'll have a real reason to fight.'

'Yes, of course—things are different now that we have each other. You will keep safe, won't you?'

He held me close to him. I was suddenly very frightened—frightened for his life. We

44

walked on in silence for a while. I hoped that he would not sense my fear.

'You haven't told your father about me yet, have you?' he asked, after some time.

'No, not yet,' I replied, grateful that the subject of war had been dropped.

'That's another thing I didn't consider . . . you see . . . my gran was right about me.'

'Mm?'

'When I started walking out with you, I didn't think about the difference in our backgrounds.'

'Neither did I! And that's because it isn't of any importance.'

'Yes it is, Elizabeth. You're a wealthy lady and I have nothing. You can't tell me that your father will welcome me into your family—he's no doubt got some rich, young gent from the nobility marked out for you.'

'Well, he'll have to realize that the only person I will ever marry is you—won't he?'

'He'll probably disown you and throw you out with no money at all!'

'So what?'

'SO WHAT? You'll have a very different life as my wife, from the one you've had as his daughter. You're used to servants and beautiful things all around you . . . and all that space!' David looked towards Maramar Grange. 'I can never give you all those things.'

'Good! I'm glad. I don't like my way of life. Most of the time I feel useless and rather silly.'

'Elizabeth!'

'We'll rent a little house and . . . and I'll take in washing to earn extra money.'

David chuckled.

'There won't be any need for that,' he said. 'I can earn a fair wage as a carpenter when the war is over.'

'Well then—what are you worried about?'

'I don't like the idea of you falling out with your family because of me.'

'Perhaps I won't. Father's been different since my mother died. He doesn't seem to care much about anything anymore. I expect he'll see how happy we are together and agree that we should be married.'

'I doubt that very much.'

'Let's not worry about it now. I'll choose a good moment to introduce you to him . . . when he seems a bit brighter.'

'All right—if you say so. Don't leave it too long though.'

I knew in my heart that Father would not accept David as my husband. This was not the right time, however, to confront the problems that would doubtless arise when he was told of our courtship.

*   *   *

David and I were in love—I wanted that to fill my world—nothing else.

'I have to tell my father about David

sometime,' I explained to Jenny a few days later. 'He won't be very happy about it, but he's got to know. I can't decide whether to break the news . . . no, that isn't strictly truthful . . . I can't pluck up enough courage to tell him.'

'Perhaps he'll accept it,' Jenny replied hopefully. 'You said yourself that he's changed a lot since your mother died. He's certainly been very docile as far as we're concerned—below stairs, I mean.'

'This is a little different though, Jenny. To announce that I want to marry a private in the army, when Father has always planned to pair me off with some boring, upper-class fool . . . well . . . he isn't going to give us his blessing, is he?'

'Why don't you wait till you're older, Elizabeth? Then you can marry whoever you want to and he won't be able to stop you, will he?'

'I won't let him stop me now! Mm . . . perhaps I will wait a bit longer though. David will be back in France soon, after all. Yes . . . that'll be best . . . I'll talk to Father about it when David comes home again. Perhaps if I introduce them, and Father sees what a pleasant young man David is . . .'

'It'll all work out for the best.'

'I hope so. I know one thing, though, Jenny . . . I'm going to marry David, whatever Father says. I'll never wed anyone else, and that's for sure.'

At the end of July came the news that I had dreaded. David was to return to France. The light was to go out of my life.

We wanted to spend the evening before his departure together, so I arranged to meet him at the main gates of Maramar Grange after dinner. I told Father that I had a headache and wanted to go to bed early. He believed my lie without question.

I went down the servants' stairs, through the woods and out of the huge wrought-iron gates which marked the boundary of our land.

David was waiting. I took him by the hand and led him through the gates. We followed the railings round to the rose garden, where we could sit and talk, protected from the curious eyes of others by its high walls.

The perfume of the flowers wafted on the warm, evening air, and the setting sun lent a restful, mellow glow to the world.

I remember how I buried my head against David's chest and cried because I could not bear the thought of being without him. He held me close to him but now, as well as his usual tenderness, I felt desire in his embrace.

His arms were strong against my body and he pressed his lips passionately on mine. As he held me tighter and his breath came hot and panting on my neck, I knew what was happening, but I had no wish to stop it. We sank down onto the grass and David made love to me.

I felt feminine and complete. I wanted nothing in this world but him. I wondered how life could be so cruel as to take him away from me.

We lay together in silence, simply enjoying each other's closeness, until it was time for him to leave.

'Take this, Elizabeth,' he whispered, pushing a wide, gold band onto my finger. 'It was my mother's. I want you to keep it always ... whatever happens.'

'Oh, come back to me, David ... please come back,' I sobbed.

He did not.

*   *   *

Elizabeth looks down at the gold ring. Tears fill her eyes as they had done all those years ago. She cries for her youth and she cries, once again, for David.

'Is that sun too strong for you, Elizabeth?' Jennifer comes round to the front of the wheelchair. 'It's making your eyes water. I'll take you round to the shady side, shall I? We'll have to get you some sunglasses.'

Elizabeth is wheeled round the corner of the balcony to where the sun is less strong.

She can see the high walls of the old rose garden from here. Elizabeth wants to be taken inside the house. She wants to lie down.

'Everything all right?' calls the woman in the blue dress, from across the balcony.

'Yes,' Jennifer replies, 'just moved Elizabeth out of the sun, that's all.'

'Good idea.'

'It'll soon be time to go in for lunch,' Jennifer says to Elizabeth. 'Then I expect you'd like to rest on your bed for a while.'

Jennifer understands.

Elizabeth stares at the walls of the old rose garden and remembers.

*　　　　*　　　　*

There was no telegram for me—no notification—I was not his wife after all.

It was the end of September when Jenny came to my room and broke the devastating news to me. She had received a letter from Stanley, that morning, telling her of David's death.

I could not cry . . . not at first.

'Will you walk with me, Jenny?' I whispered. 'I can't bear to stay in here. I want to be outside in the air. I feel that I shall suffocate in this house.'

'Er . . . yes . . . of course.'

'Don't worry, I'll tell cook that I delayed you.'

I needed Jenny with me.

We walked through the orchards to the rose garden. It was as though I were drawn to that

50

special place, where David and I had known so much love. Once within its walls, I began to cry.

Jenny knew that no words could console me, but her serene presence was a comfort. We sat together for some time, until my eyes burned and my throat ached and I could cry no more.

'Did Stanley say what happened?' I asked. 'Was he with David?'

'He was there . . . yes. David didn't suffer . . . not at all.'

'How did he die, Jenny?'

'Well, in battle. I don't know exactly what happened, I'm afraid. Stanley didn't go into any great detail.'

'Was he fighting? Did Stanley say that David was fighting the enemy?'

'He must have been, Elizabeth. They're all fighting the enemy, aren't they?' Jenny looked bewildered.

'I wish I knew.'

'Here, read Stanley's letter.'

Jenny took the folded sheet of paper from her apron pocket.

'. . . terrible news . . . David was killed in action yesterday. I know it will be difficult for you, but please tell Elizabeth. Explain to her that he died instantly—there was no pain.'

'I'm glad Stanley was with him. Perhaps he'll be able to tell me when he comes home again.'

'Tell you what?'

'I want to know. Oh, Jenny—it's nothing you can help me with. It's something that David talked about. It seems desperately important now.'

*   *   *

For days and weeks I walked about the house, hardly conscious of what was going on around me. I could share my grief with no one but Jenny, and even she was unaware of how I was agonizing over the circumstances of David's death. Had he defended himself? Or had he, once again, been too petrified to fight for his own life—and for our future together? I needed to know. Surely his love for me had given him something to live for. And now, now that I knew I was carrying his child . . . oh, if only he had known!

My mourning was like a great weight upon me. It obliterated everything else from my mind. I was scarcely aware of the daily nausea from which I was suffering. Even the thought of my father finding out that I was pregnant failed to penetrate the deep sense of loss which shrouded me in its melancholy veil.

By the end of October, however, I began to realize that decisions would have to be made. I would not be able to hide my fullness of figure for very much longer.

Though I was sure that I would always grieve for David, I knew that the time had

52

come for me to consider his unborn child. The baby must be my priority now.

*   *   *

'I'm going to have David's baby,' I confided to Jenny one day when my mind was in turmoil over what I should do.

'Elizabeth!' My friend was clearly stunned.

'Don't be disapproving, Jenny, please,' I begged. 'No one else will understand, but I thought you might.'

'I'm not being disapproving . . . but what will you do, Elizabeth?'

'I've got no idea—well, at least, I didn't have. I'm beginning to see, however, that there aren't many options open to me. I think I shall have to leave home—run away, I suppose.'

'I'll come with you!'

Jenny's first reaction was just what I expected from my most loyal friend.

'Jenny . . . think . . . you can't come with me. I'll have a struggle to keep myself—I'd never be able to pay you. What about your mother and brothers—what would they do? They depend on you.'

'But I can't let you go on your own! Where will you live?'

'I'll be all right. I'll have to get a job and rent a room.'

'You must tell your father, Elizabeth. I'm sure he wouldn't throw you out. He'd be angry

53

at first, of course, he's bound to be. He'd calm down, though. He wouldn't force you to leave your home!'

'He would! His only daughter expecting a baby and the father is a private in the army—what a disgrace! Believe me, Jenny, he'd have no sympathy. All he would think about would be the scandal—the good name of the family being brought to the level of the gutter! I can hear him now! I'd have to leave—he'd disown me. I think I would rather just go quietly.'

'But you shouldn't go off all alone!'

'I'll write to Edward and tell him that I'm leaving home, but I won't say why.'

'Elizabeth, please—let me come with you! Let me look after you!'

'You can't, Jenny. I'll keep in touch. Don't worry about me.'

'I shall—of course I shall!'

Over the next few days, I gathered together the clothes and possessions that I wished to take with me.

A letter came by return of post from Oxford. Edward had sent me fifty pounds, saying that if I must be so foolish as to leave home, at least I'd have something to live on for a while. I wrote and thanked him.

That was the last contact I ever had with my only brother.

I felt so ill as I prepared to leave the safety and comfort of my home that I wondered if I would have the strength to go. I knew only too well, however, that there was no other way. My nausea was getting worse. Everything I ate made me dreadfully sick and I was worried that my baby was not being properly nourished. Milk was the only thing that I could keep down, so I drank as much as possible, in the hope that my child—David's child—would grow strong inside me.

While I was making plans for the exact moment of my departure, my father announced that he was going to London for a few days to visit a friend. I decided that this would be the ideal time for me to leave Maramar Grange.

*　　　*　　　*

Father kissed me on the forehead.

'I'll see you on Friday, Elizabeth,' he said, his usual stern tone stifling any sign of the fondness that may have lived in his heart. 'You look a bit peaky. Make sure that you eat properly.'

'Yes, Father.'

'Goodbye.'

'Goodbye, Father.'

I watched him from the window as he drove away. It occurred to me that I may never see him again, and tears, quite unexpected tears, ran down my face. There had been much contention between us. I had never really felt close to this strictest of men, yet there I was, regretting our parting. I decided that my emotions were heightened, because of David's death and my own condition. I felt my tears to be irrational. I could not deny, though, that somewhere deep in an unidentifiable part of me, there was a small voice that cried out to my father. I suddenly knew that I would miss him.

'Please, Elizabeth,' Jenny implored, when I went to say goodbye, 'go to Gossborough. My mother will give you a roof over your head—you know that.'

'I can't burden her with my troubles, Jenny, she has enough of her own.'

'She'll look after you though. And I can see you whenever I visit home. Please, Elizabeth, do as I say!'

'Look, I'll go to Gossborough and search for a room. I've got Edward's fifty pounds . . . I wish I were old enough to claim some of my own money, but Father will make sure that I don't get any of that now that I have let the family down so badly. Anyway, with Edward's money, I can rent a room somewhere near to your house. Then I can see you when you visit Gossborough.'

'Well, that'll be something, I suppose.'

'If it weren't for the baby, I would go to your mother, Jenny—I know she could do with the rent. As it is, though, I'd rather be with complete strangers—I can't quite explain why. And your mother hasn't got a spare room, has she? I don't really want to share a room, Jenny. You do understand, don't you?'

'Of course. Do take care though—and go to her if you can't find anywhere.'

'It's quite a challenge, when you think about it, Jenny. I'm going out into the world to fend for myself. I just wish that it were David and I together.'

'I know.'

'I shall look for a job, of course.'

'You will see a doctor, won't you, Elizabeth? You might need help when the baby comes.'

'Yes, I'll see a doctor, don't worry about that—I'll be fine.'

'I'm visiting Mother next Wednesday, so I'll meet you there—please come—then you can give me the address of your room.'

'All right, I'll see you on Wednesday then. There, it isn't really like saying goodbye at all, is it?'

'I'll miss you so much, Elizabeth. This place will be awful without you.'

'I must go, Jenny—the quicker, the better.'

My friend hugged me tightly—once again the tears flowed. I reprimanded myself and decided that I must behave in a more mature manner. Now that I was an independent woman, I would have to be tougher.

Jenny said that she would take one of my bags to her mother's, so that I had only a small case to carry to the station. The lane that led away from Maramar Grange had never seemed as long as it did on that day. I did not allow myself to wonder what would happen to me.

As the train transported me, steadily and dependably to Gossborough, I looked out at the countryside in its autumn garb. The trees, with only the most persistent of leaves still clinging on to their branches, looked naked and barren, while beneath them, the fronds of the densely growing ferns moved in the breeze like a thousand waving hands.

The rhythm of the train made me feel drowsy, but I was afraid of missing my stop so I forced my eyes wide open.

*　　　*　　　*

Once in Gossborough, I began at the market-square and walked along each road which led off from it, in search of a room to let.

As the time passed it grew colder. I could hardly keep my fingers round the handle of my case because they were so numb. I decided to go to the tea-shop where I had met David and Stanley for the first time. It was warm in there and I pressed my hands around my hot cup of tea in order to get the feeling back.

There were only a couple more streets for me to try. I was beginning to fear that I would not find anywhere to stay. I set off again, knocking at doors and asking passers-by if they knew of a room to let. The tea had made me feel sick and I was becoming so tired that I could scarcely put one foot before the other.

At the corner of Prince's Lane I just had to rest. I put down my case and sat on it. Perhaps Jenny's mother would know of someone who would take me in. I was tired and cold and very lonely—yes, I would ask Mrs. Todd. My breath lingered, like mist, on the bitter air. I rubbed my hands together and pulled my coat tightly around me, in preparation for the walk along Prince's Lane.

As I stood up, however, a hand rested on my shoulder and I turned to see a woman standing there, staring at me. She was tall and thin, about fifty-five years old and, for a moment, I considered her to be frightening. Her grey hair was scraped back in a bun, but a few wayward wisps around her hairline blew about in the wind. She had a large, pointed nose and her chin was too pronounced for the rest of her face. As she looked at me with anaemic blue eyes, I can remember thinking that she was strangely witch-like.

'You look as if you could do with a good, hot meal, lass,' the woman said in a kindly voice which belied her intimidating appearance.

'Er, yes . . . I . . .'

'Come on then.'

The stranger's unfamiliar northern accent seemed to caress my aching mind. She guided me into the first house in Prince's Lane. I was so weary that I had neither the inclination nor the strength to argue with her. She showed me into her front room, where a fire glowed in the grate. After the raw elements outside, the warm atmosphere of the woman's home intoxicated me.

'Thank you,' I murmured, as she took my case from me and pointed to an armchair.

'I'm Mrs. Tillerton, but everybody calls me Tilly,' she said, with a benevolent directness. 'I don't want to know your business, lass, but you look to me as if you need a helping hand. Would you like to stay here for a while—or have you got to get yourself off home?'

'No—er—I'm looking for a room to rent—I've got plenty of money!'

'We'll not worry about money yet. Let's get some colour back to those cheeks first, shall we? I've got some soup on. You sit there and warm yourself—I'll bring it to you.'

'Oh, thank you so much,' I whispered, unable to believe my good luck.

That night, I slept in Tilly's spare bedroom. I was woken, at two o'clock in the morning, by the most sharp and cramping pains in my stomach. Tilly heard my cry and came to me. She looked after me like a mother would have done, with no word of disapproval passing her pale, thin lips.

I lost David's child that night. My body expelled it as though it were something alien and unclean, but it was not . . . it was my baby.

I cried on Tilly's shoulder until dawn.

*　　　*　　　*

The next day, I was fed on nourishing food and comforted by that wonderful woman.

I grieved for my baby and I feared that, wherever he was, David might know that I had not been able to bear his child. This thought haunted me for some time until, as I lay there regaining my strength, I began to deliberate on my beliefs—on the likelihood of there being life after death. I had often doubted the existence of a God, but now I was more certain than ever before that there was no such being. How could a God who cared for mankind allow such misery? How could he permit wars to happen and babies to die? No . . . there was no afterlife . . . no heaven . . . David was gone and so was our child. I was desolate.

It was several days before Tilly would let me get up. She took a message to Mrs. Todd's house giving Jenny my address, so that my friend was able to visit me.

I was so fortunate to be in Tilly's care. Jenny brought me sympathy and her usual kindness, but Tilly was like a rock—a rock on which I could lean and depend.

As my body grew strong again, I began to put my grief to one side and to think of my future. It was not easy, but I knew that I must.

61

Tilly had been very good to me and I wanted to repay her properly for all she had done.

'You've got a home here for as long as you need one, lass,' she told me, when I was up and about again.

'I want to get a job, Tilly,' I explained. 'Then I can pay you in full for my room and my food. You've been so kind. I truly don't know what I would have done without you.'

'God always provides a friend when you need one,' Tilly replied, smiling.

'Oh . . . does He?'

I hope that I hid my disbelief.

*   *   *

The next time Jenny visited me, she brought a letter from Stanley. She had written and told him that I was worried about the way in which David had died, and that if he could put my mind at rest in any way, she would be grateful. The post, especially that going to and from the battlefields of Europe, was very sluggish. Now that Stanley's letter had arrived, I was almost afraid to read it. I knew I had to, though. I was sure I would have no peace until I knew. Alone in my room, I prepared myself for the truth.

*   *   *

'. . . as I said in my other letter David died

62

instantly. Please assure Elizabeth, once again, that he did not suffer any pain. He was shot in the back. He cannot have known that the enemy soldier was behind him.'

'Shot in the back,' I reflected, 'he was running away. Poor, dear David—he was simply too gentle and too good for this world. Even my love did not give him reason enough to defend himself.'

The following day, I went to look for work. I knew now exactly what I wanted to do. I walked a short way out of town to the Gossborough Infirmary, where I enlisted as a trainee nurse.

*   *   *

Over the next few years, I learned to care for the sick. Jenny was inclined to think that my father knew where I was, but he never tried to find me or to contact me and, during that time, I never returned to Maramar Grange. I lived instead with Tilly. My work at the infirmary both occupied me gainfully and gave my life a purpose.

When my training first began, however, I wondered if I would be able to cope with the situation in which I found myself. I had never before taken orders in the way that I was now expected to. The ward sisters were, at best, officious and, at worst, downright bad tempered.

I watched the way in which the other young nurses accepted the discipline of their chosen career and, though I frequently longed to ask my superiors just who they thought they were talking to, I learned to think only of the patients which, in time, helped me to achieve a state of some humility.

When I had first visited Jenny's home, the idea of working for one's living had seemed hard, yet almost romantic to me. Now that I had actually left my advantaged lifestyle, however, I must admit that the transition to a full time job was anything but easy.

Though nursing was the only work I wanted to do, the first few months of my training were extremely traumatic for me. I wanted to minister to the sick and old, to mop the fevered forehead and give solace to those in pain. In fact, I spent most of my time making beds, cleaning up vomit and running to the beck and call of my superiors.

As the months passed, though, my determination to succeed at my work was rewarded. Gradually, I was given more specialized medical tasks to perform, whilst newcomers took on the more menial, but very essential, side of the job. Even then, I found the work terribly demanding and often harrowing. I remember fainting clean away the first time I saw, and smelt, a gangrenous wound, and I cried for hours when a small child died in my arms.

It was a little boy about the same age as my own son would have been. I always thought of the child, which David and I had made as a boy—I do not know why. When I watched little Georgie die, though, it was like losing my own baby all over again

The longer I worked at the infirmary, the more human suffering I witnessed, the more my conclusion that there was no God was reinforced. A God who cared for people would not let such dreadful pain and misery afflict seemingly innocent folk. No more would he permit the hideous carnage of war to go on.

My beliefs became very simplistic at this stage of my life. You were born and you died. There was nothing before conception or after death. In between, though, you should do as much for your fellow man as possible. That was my philosophy and I endeavoured to live by it.

When I reached the end of my training, I felt that a little self-congratulation was in order. My life at Maramar Grange seemed to be a part of the far distant past. I was now a member of the working class and proud to be so. I had left that futile existence which I had experienced in my young life, far behind me and, even if I had had the choice, I would not have wanted to return to it . . . not permanently anyway.

I still kept in touch with Jenny, though my hours at the infirmary prevented me from seeing her as often as I would have wished.

Stanley survived the war and, one summer's day in 1920, I attended their wedding.

Standing in the church between Tilly and Mrs. Todd, I could do nothing to hide my tears. Though I tried to tell myself that they were tears of joy, shed for my best friend and her new husband, in all honesty I knew that I cried for myself and David, and what we might have shared.

*   *   *

During those years with Tilly, I learned much about the world outside Maramar Grange . . . and even more about true kindness.

I could never bring myself to tell her that I had no faith, as such a confession would have hurt her dreadfully. Knowing Tilly, though, I was sure that she would never have shown disapproval to this heathen that she had taken in and mothered.

*   *   *

It was in the spring of 1922 when I first noticed that Tilly looked unwell. Her tender eyes became clouded and she was quiet and preoccupied. Then, one morning when I rushed into the kitchen unexpectedly, I found her stooped and gripping her side, obviously in great pain.

'What is it, Tilly?' I asked, the fact that I should be leaving for the infirmary momentarily deserting me.

'Just a bit of cramp, lass. I get it sometimes—it'll soon pass.'

Tilly straightened up and tried to hide her distress from me.

'I think you should go to the doctor's, Tilly,' I urged, trying to sound more like a concerned friend than a nurse.

'For goodness' sake, Elizabeth, the poor man's got enough to do without me troubling him about a bit of cramp!'

I knew that Tilly would brook no argument. Her use of my Christian name was always her kindly way of telling me that she was adamant.

'If the pain comes back again, you must go to see the doctor,' I replied, with as much authority as I could muster.

'Mm,' she grunted. 'You'll be late for work, lass, if you don't hurry.'

I had no alternative but to let the subject drop and get myself off to the infirmary as quickly as possible.

It was only a week or two later, however, that I found Tilly crying in her bedroom and clutching her side. I sat beside her on the bed and gently pushed her hands away.

'Let me see, Tilly,' I whispered.

The lump that I felt in her side was as big as an orange.

'I'll be better in a minute,' she uttered, as

67

though concerned for my feelings.

'Why didn't you tell me before, Tilly?' I murmured.

'Because I knew you'd fuss, lass.' She took a deep breath. 'I don't want any fuss.'

'I'm getting the doctor, 'Tilly, and that is that!'

This time I would hear no argument.

An hour later Doctor Davis stood by Tilly's bed and told her that she had a tumour.

'Well, I'd guessed that,' she replied smiling. 'And don't tell me that I should have come to see you sooner, because I wouldn't have let those surgeons at the infirmary cut me open then, any more than I will now.'

'They might still be able to help you, Tilly,' I pleaded. 'Isn't that so, Doctor Davis?'

'Yes—very possibly—we'll need to take a look inside though, Mrs. Tillerton. Then we can see exactly what needs to be done . . . and do it . . . otherwise . . .'

'Otherwise I'll die.'

Tilly took my hand. I wanted so badly to cry, but I had to be strong for her sake. I reminded myself that I was used to such situations—a professional.

'Yes, Mrs. Tillerton,' Doctor Davis answered, with amiable candour. 'You really must let us help you, or you will die.'

I gripped Tilly's clammy hand and faced her squarely.

'You must let the surgeons treat you,' I

begged. 'Please—I'll be there, at the infirmary with you. I'll stay with you all the time.'

'No, Elizabeth, I'll have no knives cutting into me.'

'But . . .'

'No, Elizabeth.' Tilly closed her eyes. It was clear that the pain was intense. 'If you could give me a little something for the pain, Doctor Davis, that'll be a great help.'

'You're being stubborn. Mrs. Tillerton,' the doctor said, 'but yes, of course I'll give you something that will ease the pain—for the time being anyway.'

'Tilly . . .' I began. feeling that I wanted to hold her and hit her all at once.

'Don't nag at me, lass,' she whispered. 'I'm not in the least afraid to meet my maker. If he wants me, then I'm ready to go.'

'Oh, Tilly!' I began to cry. My professionalism could no longer be maintained.

'I don't believe in interfering with God's will,' she went on emphatically. 'So, I'll hear no more about operations and the like.'

'Damn God's will!' I shouted, causing Tilly and the doctor to stare at me in utter disbelief.

'God will forgive you for that, lass,' Tilly sighed, a warm smile bringing her eyes alive. 'It's only because you're upset that you say such things. But you mustn't be upset—not for me—I'm going to glory—I'm not frightened— not in the least. You mustn't grieve, lass. I want no sorrow.'

Doctor Davis left the house, giving me something for Tilly to take for her pain, and trying to comfort me with what seemed like well-practised platitudes.

No amount of argument from me or the doctor would persuade Tilly to enter the infirmary for surgery. Once I had accepted this, the business of watching her die became a more tranquil process, but no less sorrowful.

Her faith was so strong that she bore everything she suffered with a dignity and a bravery, which made this terrible time as easy as it could be for both of us.

'I've been thinking, lass,' she said, one bright morning a few weeks before her death. 'I'm sure the landlord would have no objections to you taking over my tenancy when I'm gone. You've got a regular job—his rent would be there each week—what do you think?'

'Let's not talk about it,' I replied.

'Don't be so silly, Elizabeth. Such things need to be sorted out. You've never told me about your family, and I wouldn't pry, but you do seem to be alone. And I thought . . . well . . . this house isn't too far from the infirmary. Do you want me to speak to the landlord about it when he comes tomorrow?'

'No, no, Tilly. I don't know what I'll do when . . .'

'When I'm gone, lass,' she put in. 'Well, I'll

tell you one thing you won't do—you won't sit and mope and cry—promise me that.'

'I . . . I . . .'

'Yes?' She grinned with an impishness that I had never before seen in her eyes.

'I promise,' I said, returning her smile and feeling wonderfully close to her.

'I shall be watching you to make sure you're getting on with your life, you know.'

We caressed and I kissed her bony, wrinkled cheek.

It was at that moment that I felt envious of Tilly—oh not of her ghastly illness—never that—but of her absolute faith. There she was, drugged and dying in terrible pain, but elated at the thought that she was going to 'meet her maker'. She was so sure—so safe—because of her beliefs, that I wished I could share her faith with her, but I just could not.

Tilly, however, died still believing that I was a Christian. I held her hand as she passed peacefully away; the pain seemed to leave her at the end. Though I could not pray for her, I hoped fervently that she would find her paradise.

I stayed on in Tilly's house until after the funeral. She had no family, so only her neighbours and myself mourned in the little church in Gossborough.

I knew that I had lost the best friend I had ever had. I felt completely alone.

On the day before Tilly's funeral, my loneliness overcame my common sense and I found myself on the two thirty train, heading out of Gossborough and towards Maramar Grange.

It was a hot, stuffy day at the end of August, and a few flashes of distant lightning gashed the sky like a huge silver sword.

As the train passed through the countryside, which lay abundant with ripening fruits and splashed with the colours of wild flowers, I tried to rationalize my thoughts. Why, on this particular day, did I feel the need to see my father and brother, and my lovely old home? I was lonely because of Tilly's death, of course, and I knew that my grief would be with me for some time, but there was more to it than that. It was as though I needed to touch my past.

Since Jenny and Stanley had moved to Southend, there was no one in my life from my days at home—no one at all. My friends and colleagues at the infirmary were all a part of my new life away from Maramar Grange. Today I needed to go back and to be with my own flesh and blood, whatever Edward and Father might think of me.

Suddenly, I was panic-stricken. What was I thinking of? Father's face was there in my mind's eye—outrage and contempt vying for domination. I knew that he would not want to see me. Edward would be changed too. No longer the childhood playmate—or the adolescent companion, who teased and joked. He would hate me for sure.

I could not face them. At the next station, I would leave the train and catch the next one back to Gossborough.

When I stood up to leave the train, though, I realized just how intimidated I was . . . intimidated by the thought of my own family and what they felt about me.

I sat down again, stubborn determination displacing my fears. Was I ashamed of my past? Was I conscience-stricken about my love for David? No. Why should I fear facing my own father? Why should I consider his feelings and Edward's? What about my needs and feelings? I wanted to go home and to see them both again—and I would do exactly what I wanted to.

As I walked up that so familiar lane towards the gates of Maramar Grange, I decided that their disapproval would not bother me. I would confront them confidently and with grace. After all, I had much to be proud of. I would tell them of my worthwhile profession, of how I had trained to be a nurse and how I was paying my own way in the world. I would make them understand that I was not asking them for money.

My courage rose. Yes, I would face my relatives as an equal. I was not returning to

Maramar Grange to ask for forgiveness, or to ask them if they would take me back. I was an independent woman now. I only wanted to see them again . . . and my old home too.

The dainty pink flowers of the willow herb, which grew in profusion all along the hedgerow, took my attention for a moment. As I stopped to admire their delicate beauty, a horse trotted past me. I turned and saw that the rider was Edward. Hesitantly, I raised my hand and tried to call but the feeble sound which passed my lips did not reach the ears of that proud young man sitting high in his saddle . . . or did it? Had he really not recognized me? I know that my back had been turned towards the lane as he approached, but surely he had seen me . . . known me.

I watched as Edward, just a few yards ahead of me, turned out of the lane and into the drive of Maramar Grange. I could not call to him again. My voice froze deep in my throat.

A few minutes later, when I reached the huge iron gates which were situated just a little way along the drive, I stood and watched Edward disappearing round the side of the house to the stables.

Suddenly, the years of my absence seemed like a barrier which could not be crossed.

There it stood—Maramar Grange—my past. I only had to go through the gates and up the drive and I would be there . . . but instead, I turned and walked away.

74

I knew now that I could not go home.

On my return to Gossborough, I felt empty and isolated.

After Tilly's funeral, I would move away—transfer to another hospital—make a new start. I must try to think only of the future—to dwell on the past would be futile.

I must be strong.

*　　*　　*

Elizabeth is frustrated by her ailing body—more frustrated than usual.

She wants to see all of Maramar Grange, to walk from room to room, from memory to memory, alone and unaided. She wants to spend time in her past and find what is here. All she has, however, is limited access, determined by someone else's will—never her own.

Elizabeth closes her eyes. She must know the house again. She will use her mind to revisit.

The dining room, that was the centre of her home and of her family life in her youth. She tries hard to picture it. The images grow stronger and more precise in her irrepressible mind.

There it is—yes—she sees again the richly patterned, burgundy carpet, which covered most of the well-trodden floorboards, and which fascinated her as a child. She

75

remembers sitting on a small, velvet stool beside the fire and allowing her fingers to follow the carpet's intricate design. In the centre of the room stands the long dining table, which is so highly polished that it reflects the dazzling chandelier like a mirror.

Elizabeth can see the beautiful room so clearly now. She feels one of the staff tuck in the blanket which covers her legs. They think she is asleep. If she opens her eyes, she may lose her memories, so she keeps them shut.

She feels content and safe in her past. Her reminiscences give her a reason to go on. There is more than that though. She feels that she must search, so that she can learn all that her old home has to tell her.

A special time comes to Elizabeth's mind— a Christmas—but no. Suddenly she feels panic. She opens her eyes wide. This memory is not one that she wishes to relive.

Elizabeth has no choice now, though. She closes her eyes in acquiescence.

*　　　*　　　*

I was eight years old—possibly nine—and unable to contain my excitement because it was the day before Christmas Eve.

Nanny had gone to deliver Christmas presents to her family, leaving Mother, Edward and myself to finish decorating the rooms. Father was busy on the estate.

Edward was up on a small stepladder arranging holly over the ghastly portrait of my great grandfather, which hung over the fireplace in the dining room, whilst Mother and I hung paper lanterns on the Christmas tree.

'Shall I try and cover his face up with the holly?' Edward suggested, cheekily pointing to the portrait.

'Don't let your father hear you say things like that, Edward,' my mother scolded, trying to smother a smile, 'he was very fond of his grandfather.'

'What a face, though!' Edward exclaimed, causing me to giggle loudly.

'Edward!' Mother snapped. 'Enough!'

Whilst Mother sorted through the box of decorations, Edward and I attempted to laugh silently, but when my brother tried to mimic the expression on the face of our grim ancestor, my mirth exploded noisily from my throat.

'Elizabeth, don't be silly,' Mother said, becoming impatient. 'Both of you settle down.'

Edward started to set up the nativity scene, which stood, every year, on a small table next to the dining room fireplace.

'Get the clean straw for the stable,' Edward ordered, looking sternly at me now.

'Don't be bossy!' I retaliated.

'Stop arguing!' Mother put in.

'Well, he didn't even say please!' I

explained, as though deeply wounded by my brother's rudeness. 'And I don't want to get the straw anyway; I want to get the people out!'

I pushed Edward out of the way and grabbed one of the perfectly crafted plaster figures from the wooden box, which housed them between Christmases. At this point in the proceedings, Edward shoved me back—only rather harder than I had been able to shove him. I tripped over my feet and the little figure flew out of my hand and landed heavily on the dining table.

Edward and I stood in petrified silence as Mother rushed to inspect the broken Virgin Mary.

'Oh no!' she gasped. 'It'll never mend—it's in too many bits! And look at the table—it's made a dent where it landed—it's scratched the surface! Oh, Elizabeth, how could you be so silly?'

'Edward pushed me!' I squealed, the tragic tears of childhood running down my cheeks.

'She pushed me first!' Edward shouted, not quite crying, but almost.

'Stop shouting—both of you!' Mother insisted. 'What am I going to tell your father? His mother had those nativity figures made for him when he was a boy—and just look at the table!' She turned to me. 'Elizabeth—the safest place for you to be is in your room, I think.'

She pointed to the door.

'But, Mother!' I implored. 'I want to do the decorations with you!'

'Go to your room, Elizabeth, and stay there!'

She pointed again.

'What about Edward?' I argued, with near hysterical indignation. 'Isn't he going to his room too?'

'Don't question me, Elizabeth.' Mother was very agitated. 'Nanny told me recently that you were becoming too wilful, but I didn't really take too much notice of her until now. Not another word, please—go to your room at once!'

I ran up the stairs, crying hysterically. Once in my room, I threw myself on the bed, kicking my feet tempestuously and pounding the pillows with my clenched fists.

It was ruined! That wonderful day, which I had long anticipated, was ruined! The Virgin Mary was broken and I could not even help with the rest of the decorations.

Though I did not know for certain whether or not Edward had been sent to his room, the injustice of my banishment raged in my mind all that day.

Mother made me eat in my room too. Perhaps this was to protect me from Father's temper rather than to punish me further, but at the time it all seemed very unfair and I was absolutely wretched.

When Nanny got back, she came to

supervise my bath and see me to bed. She seemed cross with me too. Mother was still terse when she came to say goodnight and Father did not come at all, though HIS absence afforded me some relief.

Although it was as a cold December night, my skin was hot from the fury I still felt. As I tried to sleep, the frustration within me at missing my lovely day, grew to enormous proportions. I hated Edward, and my mother and father too.

It must have been about midnight when I could restrain myself no longer. I threw back the bedclothes and put on my dressing gown.

Though I was unaccustomed to being awake at this time of night, my tired body was dominated and fuelled by the passion in my mind.

Half way down the main staircase, I stopped and looked around me. The house seemed so much bigger when no one else was there, and when the darkness was absolute. I refused to be frightened, though. I continued down the stairs and then along to the dining room door.

Once inside the room, the blackness was lifted by the embers of the fire which still glowed, some golden orange and others darkening red, in the grate.

I tiptoed up to the nativity scene, which looked quite beautiful in the firelight, even though the Virgin Mary was in absentia. Its beauty seemed to make everything worse. I mused on how Edward had probably been allowed to help my mother finish the decorations and set up the nativity. I hated its special, holy loveliness.

My ferocity was intense.

Without considering the consequences, I grabbed one of the spills, which Father used to light his cigars, from the container on the hearth. I pressed it against one of the hot coals and watched it flare. My only thought was to destroy the nativity.

I held the small flame under the straw, which was spread over the floor of the miniature stable, and watched as it caught light.

To see the dry straw crackle and burn gave me considerable satisfaction. Then, the straw in Jesus's manger flared as well, and so did the wooden walls of the old stable.

The flames were fascinating—vivid, mysterious and untouchable.

It was a few minutes before flagrant reality tore me from my spellbound state. A huge flame lapped up the side of one of the heavy, velvet curtains, which adorned the windows of the dining room.

I gasped and put my hands to my mouth in horror. The realization that the fire was spreading immediately expelled all other thoughts from my mind. I began to cough, as thick, suffocating smoke billowed from the curtains—both were on fire by now. Fear and panic ran down my spine like cold slime. I must get help. Though that would mean confessing to this dreadful deed. I was far too scared to cry. My tears were born from the effects of the dense smoke.

The corner of a small, antique table, which stood in front of the windows, was also smouldering now. I knew that only one course of action was open to me.

I ran from the dining room screaming that there was a fire.

My father was the first to emerge from the bedrooms. He towered above me, staring first at the smoke, which surged through the open door of the dining room, and then at the spill, which I still grasped in my sweaty, black fingers.

Pushing me to one side, he ran down the hall and hit the dinner gong fiercely, over and over again, until the deafening noise made me wince and cover my ears with my hands.

I was no longer afraid of the fire . . . only of my father.

Immediately the house was in chaos. Servants ran up and down the hall, in their nightclothes, with buckets and pans full of water, shouting instructions to one another as they went. My father, charging around and assessing the situation as it developed, roared orders to one and all.

Edward and myself sat on the stairs until the worst of the commotion had abated.

82

My brother seemed to be enjoying the pandemonium.

'We could all have been killed,' he whispered excitedly. 'Burnt to death while we slept!'

I wanted to cry—but I would not.

After a while, when all was deemed to be safe again, Nanny took us both back to bed, having washed us and provided clean night clothes first. She did not mention the cause of the fire.

* * *

Next morning, I woke early. It took me several minutes to really take in what had happened during the night. I crept down the stairs just to make sure that it had not been a ghastly nightmare. The mingling odours of burnt cloth and damp soot were enough to assure me that it had not.

Once inside the dining room, I stared at the damage, which I had caused. In the pure but unforgiving light of day, it looked as I had always imagined that hell might look—black and ugly.

My thoughts turned to my father. I had incurred his displeasure on many occasions, but never for a deed as dire as this. What punishment would he inflict on me?

I decided that I would not wait to find out what honors I would have to endure. I would run away.

As I turned to do so, however, I bumped into my father entering the room. He took my hand and led me along the hall to his study.

'I've been looking for you, Elizabeth,' he said grimly.

I felt sick with fear.

Father sat down behind his desk. I was relieved that such a substantial piece of furniture stood between us.

'I'm so sorry, Father,' I began, hoping that a vehement show of remorse might help matters, and knowing that a denial of blame would be fertile.

'You don't have to say sorry to me, child,' he answered sternly, but without threat.

'I don't understand,' I murmured.

'Curtains can be replaced, Elizabeth, and so can furniture.'

I stared in bewildered disbelief. My father spoke quietly now—almost kindly. Where was the anger and what was the punishment?

'Please forgive me, Father,' I whimpered.

'Don't you understand, child? It is not my forgiveness you must ask . . . not this time. You have burnt the nativity . . . something which is divine and holy. You destroyed the stable and the little Jesus and that is a kind of blasphemy.'

'What will happen to me?' I gasped, absolutely petrified and wishing that I had been given a good spanking—or some other more earthly punishment.

'That is not up to me, Elizabeth. It is out of my hands. God will punish you as He sees fit.'

'What will he do to me?' I half sobbed, half shouted.

'God has many ways of dealing with those who have sinned.'

'I'll ask Him to forgive me!' I cried. 'Nanny says that God is kind and that He forgives anyone who is truly sorry for their mistakes, and I am truly sorry—really I am!'

'Oh yes, Elizabeth, God will forgive you—but he will punish you first.'

Father's face showed a kind of pleasure—a smugness because he knew that he had terrified me with his quiet words.

'I . . . I . . .' My thoughts would not come to my lips.

'Go to your room now, child,' he ordered softly, 'and stay there all day thinking about what you have done. A few prayers, asking for forgiveness, might be in order, I think.'

'But it's Christmas Eve!' I whined pathetically.

'I know,' was all he said.

I sat in my room all that day, praying for God's forgiveness and pondering on what tortures the Lord's wrath might bring upon me.

*   *   *

For many months after the fire, I waited for divine retribution. This was, of course, Father's punishment. Yes, it had been his, not God's, and it was a dreadful, lingering one. He knew that the fear I would feel all that time would be a far greater hardship for me than any pain from a spanking could have been.

Even when I was a young woman and something tragic happened, like my mother's death, or David's, I could not help thinking, albeit fleetingly, that perhaps I was being punished for burning that holy scene. By that time, however, I was almost convinced that there was no God, so I would remind myself sharply that the nativity was only a toy, and that if there was no God, how could He punish me for anything?

Mother died because she was ill and David died because he was shot.

There was no divine being involved at all.

*   *   *

Elizabeth lies on her bed. Her eyes are closed but she is not asleep.

'Shall we leave her a bit longer?' the Welsh voice asks.

'Yes, she might be dreaming beautiful dreams,' Jennifer replies wistfully.

'That's about all she's got now, isn't it—dreams?'

'Mm.'

'You know, Jennifer, when I was a girl, I used to think how wonderful it would be to make old bones. I wanted to live until I was a hundred, but not now. Seeing these poor old souls has made me change my mind about that. Once I start to lose my faculties they can put me down—like a sick dog.'

'You might change your mind when the time comes.'

'I doubt it.'

Elizabeth does not want to die. She had done, when the stroke had rendered her body an encumbrance to her mind, but not now. Now, she wants to be left alone so that she can go back. She wants to relive . . . to feel again . . . to find the answer.

This old house has allowed her to remember—shown her the way to her past. She must follow its lead, even to old heartaches. Perhaps then she will know the truth.

Suddenly the walls dividing the little rooms, in which the old folk exist are gone. Elizabeth can see the drawing room as it used to be.

Her thoughts are lured to a beautifully carved oak table, on which stand several cherished family photographs. There is her mother as a young girl and her father as a handsome soldier. Elizabeth wants to smile as she sees again Edward and herself when they were very small. They stand together in unnaturally stiff pose. The photographs are all

87

displayed in ornate, silver frames. One is larger than the rest and very special: it is of her parents, on the day they were married. Here, on this grand wedding photograph, Elizabeth's thoughts remain. She is unsure why, at first, but then she sees, in her hand, a picture of another couple on their special day; but this is a very different photograph in a very different frame.

*   *   *

It was during the Second World War—the summer of 1942. I was living in a flat in southeast London and nursing at a hospital in Woolwich.

My life at this time consisted of work, work and more work. I had been promoted to ward sister, and my profession was the only thing that mattered to me—I had nothing else.

Each day, I cycled to and from the hospital on a sturdy bicycle, which I had bought from a second-hand shop. I had never considered whether or not I could afford a small car of my own, now that I had gained promotion, because petrol was so strictly rationed at this time that owning a car was fairly pointless.

One evening, having finished work at eight o'clock, I was cycling at a leisurely pace through the streets of terraced houses which typified this part of London, when the air-raid warning sirens wailed out over the capital.

My flat was over a greengrocer's shop and I was only ten minutes from home, but I decided that a short diversion towards the nearest underground tunnel entrance would be the most prudent course of action.

I loathed every minute spent down in that claustrophobic world of comparative safety, but when the German bombers threatened, the tunnel was the place to be.

As I gained speed on my bicycle, I could hear the planes' engines moaning menacingly in the distance and then sudden eruptions of sound as they discharged their deadly, man-made hell onto more Londoners, throwing their lives and homes into the most distressing turmoil.

People emerged from their houses, pushing prams and dragging children who were too young to be evacuated and who seemed quite resigned to their lamentable lot, along the narrow pavements. Here and there, huge piles of rubble and half standing houses stood where homes used to be, revealing to every passer-by the flowery wallpaper and worn stair carpet that were once a part of some family's private world.

The planes grew louder overhead, and the frightened feet pounded faster and heavier on the paving stones. Dusk was falling at last after this warm June day. Like a protective cloak, darkness would soon cover the city.

As I approached the tunnel entrance, the

engines of a bomber roared so thunderously above me that I leapt from my bicycle and ran for cover. The little street shook as one of the houses took a direct hit. I scrambled out from the doorway in which I had sheltered and ran across to where brick dust hung like a gritty cloud in the humid air.

In only a matter of seconds, three A.R.P. wardens were at my side.

'I'm a nurse,' I said, forgetting that my uniform would speak for itself. 'If there's anyone in there, I might be able to help them.'

'Oh there's someone in there all right,' one of the wardens replied huskily, while his two colleagues started to pull back rubble from what used to be the front door. 'An old couple live here. She's bedridden and he won't go to the shelter because it would mean leaving her. I knew the poor old devils would cop it one day.'

'Is she usually upstairs?' I asked.

'No, love, she's got her bed down in the back room.'

We coughed and choked as we clambered along the hall of the house, throwing chunks of its fallen shell to one side as we went.

'Mitch!' one of the wardens called out. 'Mr. Mitchell, are you all right?'

We listened but heard nothing.

'I think the kitchen and scullery took the worst of it,' another of the men said, clearing the dust from his throat as he spoke. 'We won't get through there at all, it's completely flattened.' He guided me past a doorframe, which had fallen at an angle across the hall. 'In here, love,' he whispered, 'the old lady's always in here. You can get through—it's not too bad in there.'

I rushed to the bed, which took up almost all of the room. There was brick dust and fallen plaster on the bedspread and pillows, and on the old lady's face too, but nothing heavy had landed on her.

'Mrs. Mitchell,' I murmured, as I bent over her, but I knew that she was dead, even before I felt for a non-existent pulse. Her pretty, old eyes stared up at the damaged ceiling. I closed them. 'We can do nothing for her.' I told the warden who had entered with me. 'There are no obvious injuries. It might have been a heart attack—shock.'

'In here!' another of the wardens called from the downstairs front room.

We climbed through a hole in what had been the dividing wall between the back and front rooms of the little house.

The head and shoulders of an old man lay sticking out from under the heavy wooden dresser which had fallen on him.

'All right, Mitch,' reassured the husky voiced warden, 'we'll have this off you in a jiffy.'

At that moment, the all clear sounded and, as always, there was a sense of relief, though nobody spoke of it.

The men lifted the dresser, whilst I knelt by the old man, who was still conscious, assessing, as far as I could, the extent of his injuries.

'Where's Amy?' he asked anxiously, his eyes searching for the truth in my face, but I could not bring myself to give it.

'She's all right,' I lied. 'The back room isn't too badly damaged.'

'Tell her I'm not hurt,' he insisted, 'she'll be worried.'

I looked at the husky warden. He nodded and left the room.

'I'll tell her, Mitch,' he called back to us.

'He needs a stretcher,' I told another of the men. 'We dare not move him without one.'

'The ambulance should be here any minute, nurse. I expect they're going like mad things tonight—after that raid.'

'Don't worry, Mr. Mitchell,' I said, 'we'll soon have you tucked up in hospital.'

'What about my Amy though? She can't manage without me.'

His voice was weak and his breathing seemed erratic.

'Oh, we'll look after her,' I reassured, holding his hand, 'don't you fret about that.'

'My chest hurts,' he uttered, his face distorted because of the pain.

'Don't talk,' I urged, 'just lie still until the ambulance gets here.'

My words were not heard.

'We've never been parted, you see,' he went

on, though it was clearly difficult for him to breathe, let alone speak. 'Nearly fifty years we've been together—I don't want us to be separated now.'

'Don't worry,' I whispered, knowing that all I could offer were the usual insipid words, when so much more was needed.

A chunk of plaster fell from the ceiling at that moment, causing another cloud of dust to attack our parched and prickling throats. Mr. Mitchell started to cough, a dry, laborious cough, and blood trickled form the corner of his mouth. I feared that he would not last much longer.

'Don't let us be separated,' he pleaded in barely a murmur, as he closed his eyes.

The ambulance arrived, but too late for Mr. Mitchell.

I felt relief that he had gone. Now he and his Amy would not be separated. One would not be left to face this ugly, war-torn world without the other.

'Thanks for your help, nurse,' said the husky warden, his sombre face emphasizing the sorrow in his voice. 'I shouldn't hang around in here, love, it looks pretty safe, but you never know with bomb damage.'

'No, all right, I'll be leaving in a minute,' I answered.

I watched as Mr. and Mrs. Mitchell were carried from their home.

On the floor, by my feet, lay a little wooden

photograph frame, face down in the rubble. I picked it up. And through the cracked glass, I saw Mitch and his Amy on their wedding day. Their young faces smiled up at me through the dust and I wanted to cry—not for them though—for me. I felt selfish, yet I could not deny my feelings. I envied them all those years of love and devotion. To be that close to someone for so long seemed the most wonderful thing that could happen to a human being. How unattainable that kind of love seemed to be in my lonely life, though.

I stood the small wooden frame up against a wall—perhaps there were children—someone who would cherish it. I hoped so.

It was then that I remembered the wedding photograph on the carved oak table in the drawing room of Maramar Grange.

A pang of longing for my home and family struck at my heart for the first time in years. So strong was my loneliness at this moment, that tears washed streaks through the dust on my face and I felt so weak that I thought I would pass out. I rushed out of the house and looked around for my bicycle. I needed to be in my little flat with familiar things around me. Surely I would find comfort there, and some sense of belonging. My bicycle was gone— stolen I supposed.

After I had walked only a few steps along the pitch-black street, the air-raid warning sounded again.

'They're busy tonight!' an elderly man called to me from his front door step. 'Better get back to the tunnel!'

'Yes, I suppose so,' I replied wearily, wanting more than anything to go to my flat ... my home for one.

Once again I made for the tunnel entrance, but this time I arrived. This refuge was at least familiar, though its cramped and stale oppressiveness brought me only unwelcome familiarity, especially on such a muggy evening.

Some folk had not left the tunnel after the first raid, but had stayed put guessing, quite correctly, that another onslaught would follow.

I nodded at a few acquaintances—not friends—and sat down on a low wooden bench against the wall of this subterranean sanctuary.

My mind returned instantly, as though compelled to do so, to the silver-framed wedding photograph of my parents. How different it appeared from the Mitchells' little picture. I wished that I could talk to my mother now ... I wished that so very much.

I wondered too if my brother was still alive, or if he had been killed in the fighting. Perhaps he was alone and lonely, like me. Maybe he too thought of our childhood sometimes—of our fun and our immature love for each other. I hoped he did.

Sitting there, staring at the be-dimmed wall opposite me, my thoughts spread outward from the silver-framed photograph to the grandeur of Maramar Grange. I had taken it all for granted in my young years, and now it seemed an eternity away.

'Old Mitch and his wife copped it tonight,' a young man sitting near me informed his girlfriend, whom he held in a casual embrace, of the tragedy.

'Poor old sods,' she whined, in a tone so offensive to my ears that I wanted to yell at her to be quiet, so that I would hear no more of her voice that night.

The young man pressed his lips on hers and the two of them disappeared, thankfully, into a shadowy corner, away from the rest of the tunnel's temporary inhabitants.

It had distressed me more than I had expected, attending to the Mitchells. I knew why. Oh, I was used to injury and death—I saw it all the time at work, but that was different. When I was at the hospital, people were brought into me. I cared about them, of course, but they were patients in my domain. Being in the Mitchells' home, though, had been completely different. Seeing their possessions—their private world—had made the situation too personal for me. I had not coped well with that at all. It was as though I had intruded on their love and, although I could not have avoided this, I felt guilty because of it.

What happened next, in that ghastly

hideout, on that warm summer evening was nothing less than astonishing.

Into the tunnel came a middle aged woman, of whom I took no particular notice at first. She sat down quite near to me, and though I was occupied, at that moment, with the removal of brick dust from beneath my fingernails, I was aware that the stranger was staring at me. She slowly approached the bench where I was sitting, and a voice, so familiar yet so lodged in my past, said my name:

'Elizabeth.'

I looked up into the face of my governess— Miss Treherne—and uttered her name in a flabbergasted whisper.

Instantly I was on my feet, embracing my old teacher, something that I would never have done when she was at Maramar Grange.

We sat down together, grasping each other's hands in joy and disbelief. It was more than twenty-five years since I had seen my governess. I was only sixteen when she left my father's employment. The age difference between us then had seemed vast to me, but now that we met as mature women, the few years between us were of no importance at all.

Her hair, which had been fair in her youth, was now in the inevitable transition to grey. It was no longer piled majestically on her head, but short and wavy. The process of aging, which had manifested itself cruelly on her skin and in her bearing, had also dismissed from her eyes that spark of anticipation which had been so great a part of her charm during her time at Maramar Grange. It was as though Miss Treherne had been disappointed by her years on this earth.

After declaring our mutual pleasure at meeting again, and marvelling at the coincidence which had brought us together, we began to talk of our lives and of what had befallen us since we parted all those years before.

'I often wondered if you had married some well-to-do young gentleman,' she said smiling. 'I know that is what your father had planned for you.'

'It didn't work out quite like that,' I replied.

'No—and I'm glad in a way, Elizabeth. You are your own woman—that's easy to see—and I'm not at all surprised. I always thought of you as a wilful child—sensitive but wilful. It's good that you have a profession, and such a worthwhile one at that. You have become totally independent, and that's admirable in someone brought up in the way that you were.'

Miss Treherne's speech was still proper and her tone almost didactic.

'Independent,' I sighed, 'yes, I'm that all right.'

'Is your father still alive?' she inquired apprehensively.

'I don't know.'

My answer clearly gave cause for concern.

'Oh, Elizabeth, you've lost touch with him . . . that's so very sad.'

I felt guilty for a moment, but decided not to retain that particular emotion for very long.

'What about your family?' I asked. 'I remember you had a sister.'

'Yes. That's why I'm here. I came to visit her—she's in a local nursing home.'

'Oh dear, I'm so sorry.'

'Mm—it's her heart. She isn't too good at all. I stayed with her longer than I meant to and missed my train, and then the wretched sirens sounded and here I am. It's almost as though we were meant to meet, Elizabeth, isn't it?'

'I suppose it is—yes.'

Suddenly, Miss Treherne's genteel smile was supplanted by a desperate frown.

'Elizabeth,' she began, as though she were about to share with me a secret of grand proportions, 'I cannot miss this opportunity— probably the only one I shall ever have—to tell you something that I have never confided to another soul.'

I was intrigued, though her agonized expression prevented me from showing it.

'Well, if you want to talk . . .' I whispered hesitantly, not wishing to appear curious.

'Yes, yes, I do. More than that, I need to talk. I've carried such a burden, Elizabeth, for so many years and I'm sure that it would help to tell you everything. I know that I can trust you.'

'I'm glad you feel like that. Is it something that happened while you were at Maramar Grange?' I asked quietly.

She took a deep, fortifying breath, and looked around to ensure that no one was near enough to hear our conversation.

'I've always wondered if I caused . . . well no, it's much more than that . . . I've always blamed myself for your mother's death.'

'My mother? Why should you blame yourself for her death, Miss Treherne? It couldn't have had anything to do with you.'

'I think it might have had everything to do with me.'

'But I don't understand. Mother always seemed very fond of you. How on earth could you be responsible for her death?'

'There was an affair, Elizabeth. I betrayed her trust in the worst possible way.'

'An affair?'

'Yes, even governesses fall in love, my dear, and I loved him so very much. It was as if I had no control over what was happening. I should have stopped it—or better still, not let it start at all—I know that. When his strong arms were around me, though, that really was all that mattered—the only thing in this world of any importance at all. Can you begin to understand what I mean?'

'Oh yes, I can understand fully. And my

mother found out about it, I suppose.'

'Even worse than that, I'm afraid. She caught us together, the poor dear.'

'Oh how dreadful—dreadful for all concerned.'

'Please don't judge me too harshly, Elizabeth. If I could have saved her all that terrible distress, I would have done.'

'I'm in no position to judge anyone, Miss Treherne. I just can't bear the thought of Mother finding you and Father tog . . .'

'Oh no! No. Elizabeth—how stupid of me! It wasn't your father—it was your brother, Edward!'

'Edward?'

To try and hide my amazement would have been futile. My heart was eased, however, because I knew that Father had not been unfaithful.

'Yes. It was after his second term at Oxford. I'd always considered him to be a handsome lad, but after that short time at University, when he came home for the holidays, he was a man. I saw him in an entirely different light. At first, I tried to suppress my feelings for him; I was in a most evil dilemma. I had never known such longing, yet the shame that I felt because of my love was intolerable. There was no one I could talk to. Then, very soon, it became evident that Edward was attracted to me. The delight I felt at his attention was tempered by the fact that I knew any relationship between us would be wrong. It was not only the difference in class, that was obstacle enough, but Edward was only nineteen years old and I was twenty-nine. Elizabeth, I was at my wits' end. We began to meet and talk in the garden, usually after dusk. Then, one night, Edward declared his desire for me and he became my lover. I have never felt as wonderful since, as I did at that time. For a few weeks we met regularly—in the rose garden.'

'The rose garden?'

I repeated her words involuntarily, as I thought of David and I in that same beautiful place.

'One night, though,' she continued slowly, 'your mother was walking in the grounds. It was unusual for her to walk so late . . . but . . . she found us making love. Her expression, at that moment, will always be a vivid image in my mind. She was such a good, Christian woman. The shock which she felt turned her face to a bloodless grey. She ran sobbing from the rose garden. Next morning, your father gave me notice and Edward was sent back to Oxford, three days early, for the start of the new term. Before I left Maramar Grange, your mother became ill. A short time afterwards, cook wrote and told me that she had passed away. I have always believed that it was my fault. I never saw Edward again. I hoped that he would contact me, but he didn't.' She looked for a moment as if she might cry. 'Is he all right? Is he married?'

'I haven't heard from my brother since I was seventeen,' I answered, shaking my head with what felt like bitterness.

'Oh, I see.' Miss Treherne sounded somehow relieved.

'Don't blame yourself for my mother's death,' I pleaded.

'Her heart had never been very strong, though, and finding her son in the arms of a member of her staff—someone who was ten years his senior—must have been so outrageous to her.'

'But you aren't a wicked woman, Miss Treherne. You didn't plan all this—it happened to you—as life happens to all of us. It isn't your fault that you fell in love with Edward and he with you.'

'I should have been mature enough—strong enough—to stop the affair before it started. I'll never forgive myself for that . . . and yet, at the same time, I'm glad that I knew true love, if only for a while. I do wish that your mother hadn't suffered so because of me though.'

'Don't think like that. You and Edward probably had nothing at all to do with her illness.'

'I do feel better for telling you, Elizabeth. It's as though I've confessed and cleansed myself.'

'I'm so pleased that you told me about it. My brother seems suddenly more human. Last time I saw him he . . . he seemed very unapproachable.'

Elizabeth thought once more of the haughty young man on horseback in the lane.

'It changed my whole life, you know, that affair with Edward.'

'You have never found anyone else? I noticed that you aren't wearing a wedding ring.'

'No, there's never been anyone else, but it wasn't only that. Your father would not give me any references—quite understandably—and that meant that I couldn't get another job as a governess—or a teacher of any kind.'

'So, what have you done for a living all these years?'

'Oh, various things—cleaning mainly. And I worked in a baker's shop for a long time—I quite liked that. I did think of trying to go back to teaching a few years ago, but it's all changed now and I didn't have the confidence somehow.'

'That's sad—that it should have affected your career so badly. It's as though you've been punished for loving someone.'

'Others have a far worse time of it, Elizabeth. I mustn't grumble.'

*   *   *

That night, back in my little flat, my meeting with Miss Treherne was never out of my thoughts.

I wondered if Edward had really loved her, or if he had been unconcerned by their enforced parting. He had clearly never bothered to find her again.

Father must have been shocked by the wayward behaviour of his only son—or perhaps not. It was different for men; it always had been. Edward was rapidly bundled back to college but, apart from that, his life would have been little altered by his misdemeanour—his indiscretion. He would certainly not have found his career in ruins, like Miss Treherne had done.

Knowing Father, my erring governess had probably been labelled a whore who had led his son astray.

Life could be so unfair, and so much more so for the female of the species.

*   *   *

Elizabeth is aware of her two carers talking.

They do not know that she has been back to World War Two; they think she is dozing.

'I wonder if she wants to go to the service on Sunday morning,' Jennifer says to Denise.

'It's hard to tell what she wants. She doesn't seem able even to nod. I don't think she hears what we say to her—or maybe she hears but doesn't understand any more.'

'The vicar was asking me yesterday if I

105

could talk a few more into going along. Apparently his numbers are falling, and he does come up here specially for the old folk.'

'Mm. Well, we could wheel her along. If she isn't interested in the service she'll nod off.'

'Good idea.'

Elizabeth does not want to go to the service. She does not like priests. They should have the answer . . . they think they have it . . . but they do not. They only have empty words.

* * *

The priest who came to this house when my mother died was the Reverend Joyce. To me— I was only sixteen years old—he seemed absolutely ancient. What was left of his hair was pure white and it stuck out from under his black hat and lay around his fat, pink face in a most unruly manner. He wore a pair of small, gold-rimmed spectacles, which balanced precariously between the end of his podgy nose and its prominent bridge.

I remember him taking my hands in his. He tried to comfort me but all I could think of, as I looked into his face, was the injustice of it all.

'My mother is only young!' I cried. 'She doesn't want to die yet! She wants to be with Edward and me!'

'Perhaps she won't die,' the Reverend Joyce argued, trying to placate me in my girlish outburst.

'Have you seen her?' I demanded, as though I blamed the old man for my mother's condition.

Now that I think about it, I probably did blame him. He was the nearest I could get to this God I had grown up with.

'I have seen her, yes.'

'She doesn't look like my mother. She is white and her cheeks are hollow.'

'It is still your mother, though, Elizabeth. The outer shell of a person, which we come to know so well, is not the part that matters. It's her soul that makes your mother the person she is, and that will never change.'

'I want her here with me!' I sobbed. 'I'm not ready to lose her yet and she isn't ready to die! God should let everyone live until they're old, so that they have time to do everything they want to do, and stay with the people they love until they're ready to leave them!'

'Elizabeth, dear, you mustn't think that death is the end. Your mother is a good, Christian woman and, if—if she dies, her soul will live on with the Lord.'

'She is going to die—I know she is. And I don't think I believe in heaven. All the people that ever lived—all together in some wonderful world, with God like a king on his throne! It sounds like a fairy tale to me!'

'Yes. It does seem too good to be true, Elizabeth. I agree with you. But that's because human beings find it difficult to believe that

107

such a perfect place could exist. We are far too accustomed to this very imperfect world of ours.'

'I want to believe it. If Mother has to die, I do want to believe it.'

'Well there's nothing to stop you believing it, Elizabeth.'

*　　　*　　　*

That night, Father came to my room. He told me that Mother had passed away.

'I was with her,' he said, 'she just fell asleep. Truly, Elizabeth, she suffered no pain.'

How often I would hear those words of consolation over the next few years: Mother suffered no pain—David suffered no pain—my baby suffered no pain—even Tilly was peaceful at the end . . . but me . . . I suffered unendurable pain.

Perhaps only death is painless.

*　　　*　　　*

At Mother's funeral, I stood in the church with Edward, who had returned from Oxford to attend, and Father. They were on either side of me yet I felt totally alone.

All I could think about were the stories she would read to me when I was a little girl. I could feel again her satin dress on my skin and smell her delicate scent. I recalled how she would cuddle Edward and myself when we argued. She would tell us to say sorry to each other and then hug us both as tightly as she could.

Suddenly, I was angry. I stared at the Reverend Joyce as he approached us and, in my heart, I felt hatred.

'Why has God taken my mother?' I screamed, almost hysterical and refusing to be calmed by anyone.

'We should not question God's will, Elizabeth,' the Reverend Joyce replied, clearly uneasy that the pious atmosphere in the church had been shattered, 'even if we don't always understand it.'

'That isn't good enough!' I shouted. 'I just can't accept what you say—I can't!'

I ran out of the church and across the overgrown graveyard to Father's car, where I sat crying on the back seat whilst the chauffeur looked on helplessly.

*　　　*　　　*

It was about a year later—the following summer when I met David—before my anger began to abate.

During those first, dark months, I learned how such a disturbing emotion destroys one's very life. I realized that the only person being affected by my bitterness and my continuing fury was myself, but still I was possessed by these negative feelings. My existence became an obsessive search for a revenge that I could never achieve.

I loathed the dawning of each new day because of the utter misery I knew it would bring. Dear Jenny was kindness epitomized, but even she brought me little relief from myself.

David changed all that for a while and, even after his death, I had learned enough of life not to let that overwhelming anger return. Besides, as my belief in God diminished, I had no direction in which to channel my wrath.

*   *   *

Elizabeth is wheeled along the hall. Which room is this? The library—of course! She still thinks of it as her father's library.

The walls are no longer lined with row upon row of leather-bound books, but that huge, marble fireplace . . . yes, that is still there.

A few old folk are sitting around the room in armchairs. Elizabeth is wheeled to one of the wide bay windows, which overlook the garden.

'The vicar will be along to talk to you in a minute, Elizabeth,' Jennifer says enthusiastically. 'I'll be back to collect you when the service is over.'

Elizabeth does not want to listen to the vicar. She looks out of the window. The spinney . . . of course . . . the spinney . . . she can see the tops of the trees.

'Good morning, everyone!' the vicar chirps. 'It's a bit chilly out, but I think it'll stay dry. I hope you're all feeling well.'

Elizabeth does not hear the man of God. Her mind is trying to grasp at a nebulous event from the past, which is taunting her with its evasiveness. Why can she not quite recall? The spinney—it was there—but what? It is as though she has to fight her way back—further than ever before—through a labyrinth of memories.

Her eyes search the treetops. She takes in a sudden breath . . . she remembers.

* * *

It was late in June—a hot day. I was only six— perhaps seven years old.

We were on the south lawn, where it slopes away from the house and down to the spinney.

For Edward and myself, the spinney was a wondrous place. In the summer, we played there for hours. Sometimes it was a sweltering jungle, where we would stalk wild animals and fight with native tribes or, when we were so inclined, it was a desert, where we rode on camels and lived like Bedouins.

The spinney, with its enormous oak and beech trees, was ours. It protected us from the world, and could be transformed, by our imaginations, into anything we wanted it to be.

How sad, that with adult life comes the demise of such childhood fantasies—such glorious escape.

On that particular afternoon, Edward and I sat with Nanny, eating a picnic tea. The grass was lush and vivid and the sun's strength made it necessary for me to wear a sun-hat, which I loathed.

Across the lawn, Mother played croquet with a friend. There was much laughter from that direction, as neither lady was particularly good at the game.

A maid brought out strawberries and thick cream, which Edward and I devoured far too quickly, causing Nanny to lecture us on the merits of having good manners.

I know it was the end of June, because we had just celebrated Edward's birthday—his ninth or tenth—which fell on June the twenty-first.

He had received a beautiful brass telescope from an old aunt of ours and he was holding it to his eye, so that he could better enjoy the antics of the croquet players.

When we had eaten all we could, Nanny said that we might play for half an hour before bath time.

We ran down the gentle slope to the spinney hand in hand. It was cooler there, among the trees. The varying greens of the dense foliage contrasted, in striking manner, with the intense blue of the summer sky.

'I'll be the captain of a sailing ship, Elibeth,' Edward said, in his usual instructive tone. (When I was born, Edward was unable to pronounce my name correctly, and I remained 'Elibeth' to him for many years).

'All right,' I acquiesced.

'No—I'll be the one who climbs the mast,' he decided.

'All right,' I agreed, 'I'll be the captain then.'

'No—a girl can't be a captain,' he argued. 'Tell you what, we'll both climb the mast.'

There was one special oak tree in the spinney, which we found particularly easy to climb. The grown-ups, however, would probably have been very alarmed had they known how high we used to go.

Edward put the telescope in his pocket and climbed up first, with me following him closely. Once near the top, we each sat on a stout branch and looked around us.

'Land ahoy!' Edward shouted, 'I see strange natives on an island!'

He was looking through his telescope at Mother and her friend on the croquet lawn.

'Let me look!' I pleaded excitedly.

'Here you are then, but be careful—don't drop it!'

I held the telescope tightly and put it to my eye. The way in which this amazing instrument brought the world up close to me seemed so marvellous that I thought it must be magic.

113

'It's wonderful!' I called out, turning my attention to the house. 'Everything's so big!'

From my hideout in the tree, I could see into the library, which from the lawn was not possible. As I focused the telescope on this very bay window, I experienced what was probably the first real shock of my life. It was quite a few seconds before I could take in what was happening.

My father was standing in his library, quite close to the window, as he often did. In his arms, though, was a young woman. I stared, in bewilderment, at her auburn hair and then I watched as my father kissed her with undisguised passion. Just at that moment, as I looked, with angry disbelief at this betrayal, I heard my mother laughing, completely unaware of what was happening so very near at hand.

Though I was only young, and did not truly understand the significance of my father's actions, I knew that his behaviour was wrong.

In my distress and confusion, I dropped the telescope. My brother shouted at me furiously. I tried to scramble down out of the tree, but in my haste and with my child's mind knowing such anguish, I missed my footing. Leaves and twigs rushed past me and scratched my skin as I fell helplessly to the ground.

The next thing I remember is waking up in my bed, with Mother and the doctor looking down at me.

My head ached terribly and I was not allowed to get up for several days. I felt dreadfully sick and was given boiled fish to eat. It was awful.

When the doctor asked me exactly what had happened, I could not remember. I could recall nothing much about the afternoon except eating the strawberries and cream.

That most harrowing moment, when I had seen my father kissing that auburn haired woman, had been eradicated from my mind, perhaps because of my concussion, or possibly because I could not bear to think of it. Whatever the reason, it had never been a part of my memories—not until now.

My father—what a hypocrite! What a self-righteous hypocrite! His constantly stern attitude towards me had distanced him from me throughout my childhood. How I had needed him when I lost David and my baby. But he had made it impossible for me to confide in him about anything. How he had made me suffer when I burned the nativity! How dare he lecture me about sin! There he stood, every Sunday, in the local church, decrying all evil. He often read the lesson. While all the time, he had been deceiving my sweet mother.

The memory itself is so clear now. It is as though I have recovered a part of my life that had been lost. Yet I still find it very difficult to take in. How could he be so vile?

Perhaps his strictness was born from the fact that he had too closely encountered the sins of this world, and knew too well the weaknesses of the human animal.

*   *   *

Elizabeth looks at the vicar. He is talking about the harvest and the blessings which God bestows upon us all. She wants to shout out— to disagree—but she can only argue in her mind. Elizabeth thinks of the starving peoples of the world.

No, this man of God does not have the answer either.

Elizabeth's mind wanders from the vicar's words. Why has the memory of her father's infidelity returned to her now? It is this house . . . this room . . . the old library.

'Let us pray,' the vicar says, with habitual and predictable reverence.

Elizabeth looks out of the window. There are so many events from her past that are competing for priority in her thoughts, and nowhere more than in this room.

'Amen,' the vicar says.

'Amen,' echo the old people—all except Elizabeth.

In her nimble mind, one memory emerges. One memory, which is wonderful, yet at the same time, most terrible. It seems that it has been held back, but it is so vital to her search,

116

Now it is here though, so real in Elizabeth's thoughts.

*   *   *

During the Second World War—1943, I believe it was—I was asked to go, with six of my nurses, to work in a hospital for wounded airmen. I agreed, believing that none were more deserving of help than those poor young men injured in the fighting.

David was frequently in my mind at this time. Though I was now in my early forties and my life was devoted to my career as a nursing sister, he was still there and war made him close to me again. I cannot explain why, but I felt as though I was somehow joining him in battle as I prepared to nurse the wounded airmen. It was as if we were reunited by the adversity of war . . . or perhaps by our hatred of it.

When I received the notification of our destination, I could hardly believe what I saw before me. We were to travel to an old, empty mansion, which had been converted to a hospital for the duration of the war.

It was Maramar Grange.

For the first time in over twenty years, I was to return to my old home.

It was during the time I spent living over the shop in London and working at the Woolwich Hospital that I received this notification. I had not so much as driven past Maramar Grange since Tilly's death. I felt very apprehensive about going back but my duty came first.

No solicitor had ever informed me of my father's death, so I surmised that, if he had passed away, I had not been mentioned in his will. If this was the case, I was glad.

What of Edward, though? What had happened to my brother? I suddenly felt guilty about the fact that I had never tried to contact him. I had always thought that, like father, he would probably prefer to expunge me from his mind . . . 'the thoroughly bad lot' . . . 'there's one in every family' . . . I could hear them both saying such things. By now, of course, I knew that Edward's own past had not been without stain. Neither had Father's, for that matter, though I remembered nothing of that particular infidelity at this time.

Maybe Edward was dead too, or maybe he was away at war—an officer of course. I wondered whether I had a sister-in-law—nieces and nephews too perhaps. I thought that maybe I would get a solicitor to trace Edward one day . . . I never did.

Like my other beliefs, my faith in the strength and importance of the family had diminished over the years.

*　　　*　　　*

Maramar Grange evoked a strange mood in

me. I thought about my mother a great deal more than I had done for years, but not with sorrow or regret, not any more.

On those rare occasions when I was off duty, I would wander around the house. It was as if I was trying to bring about some deep, emotional trauma within me. I wanted to prove to myself that I was still capable of . . . of what?

Love perhaps—or passion? Nothing so intense stirred, however, during my wanderings.

Jenny's old room, up in the attic, was now a store for blankets. I stood there one day, remembering our friendship, which by now consisted only of a card every Christmas and on birthdays, and the occasional letter. She and Stanley seemed happy, though, in Southend with their three daughters, that was the main thing. I had an open invitation to go for holidays by the sea—I was always unable to go, however, for one reason or another. Family life obviously brought rewards to some. I often wondered if, being a single woman, I had been deprived of or saved from what, to me, seemed the rather doubtful joys of marriage and motherhood. Many years of life in the community had revealed to me what men and women, who had seemingly been in love at one time, could do to each other. Perhaps my all too frequent bouts of cynicism were born from bitterness or envy.

119

Whenever I wheeled a young airman out into the gardens, his legs battered, or gone altogether, I found myself thinking of David. I no longer felt that dreadful sense of loss because, at Maramar Grange, he seemed so close to me. In fact, had I believed in ghosts, I would have said that his spirit was there in the grounds, so strong was his presence.

Though it may seem that I spent my days reminiscing, in truth, my duties allowed me very little time for such personal pursuits.

I found nursing the young airmen quite different from my work in other hospitals. Perhaps I had become hardened to nursing the old and the sick. I do hope not. It was quite another matter, though, to see an otherwise healthy young body mutilated by the weapons of war.

The tragedy of it all was heightened by the obscene futility of the fighting man. I found it incomprehensible that the human race had discovered no better way of settling its differences. Had no lessons been learned from centuries of wars? From the Great War?

We would rejoice one day, when victory was ours, but these young men could never be whole again. Their tragedy was forever.

*　　*　　*

An air force chaplain used to visit the hospital and minister to those injured men who still had faith, despite everything.

The first time I met Hugh Maloney, this man of God, I am sure that I must have shown on my face the amazement which I felt and which turned my stomach, momentarily, into a block of ice. His stature, his bearing and his features were unbelievably similar to David's. If David had lived to reach his forties—I decided that Hugh was about forty-five—he would have looked exactly like this chaplain.

I tried not to stare as Hugh shook my hand and smiled at me, but I was mesmerized. When he spoke, his voice was deep and warm. There was a calmness about him, which I found simultaneously soothing and magnetic.

The library had not been converted into a ward. Instead, this was the room in which doctors, nurses and such visitors as the chaplain would meet and chat over a cup of tea or coffee.

Hugh and I would often make polite conversation after his work on the wards was completed. I avoided the subject of his faith and his vocation, until one day it became impossible for me to do so any longer.

'Are you a Christian, Sister Purley?' he asked me one afternoon when we were alone in the library.

'No,' I replied. 'I stopped being a Christian a long time ago.'

'Ah—so you started out as one!' Hugh joked, displaying none of the disapproval which I had expected.

'Yes . . . yes, I suppose I did. It's the way most people are brought up, isn't it? We are taught to believe in God.'

'I see.'

'Do you?'

Hugh seemed to be studying my face with excessive concentration. If any other man had stared at me in such a way, I would have accused him of rudeness, but with Hugh, it was somehow acceptable.

'And what made you turn against your faith, Sister Purley?' he inquired, his eyes alive with kindly curiosity.

'Elizabeth . . . please,' I insisted. 'Sister Purley makes me sound quite ancient!'

'All right—Elizabeth—why do you no longer believe in God?'

'It wasn't one isolated incident,' I explained. 'As I grew up, I suppose I refused to simply accept what I had been taught. What I saw happening in this world made me sceptical about the existence of a caring God. Perhaps it was wrong, but I began to question a lot of things in my life. No, I take that back, it wasn't wrong. I needed to question a great many things.'

'Such as?'

'Er . . . well, for a start, I had a very advantaged upbringing. My family was extremely wealthy—and for a few years I enjoyed my life the way it was. But then—then

122

I saw how others lived. People who were good and caring and hardworking but who, through no fault of their own, were poor and deprived, and always would be.'

'A lot of those poor folk—most of them, in fact—are Christians, Elizabeth.'

'Yes, I can't think why.'

'Oh dear.'

'Well, don't they see the absolute injustice of it all? How could a caring God allow some to have so much and others so little? There are other things too . . . far more important than money. How can you believe in a God who allows wars to tear His world apart and who watches millions of people killed and wounded? You still believe that there is a being—some kind of supernatural father figure—that cares for us? I'm sorry, but I can't come to terms with that at all.'

'I understand what you are feeling, but you are wrong.'

'How can you be so sure?'

'The trouble is, Elizabeth, that you don't believe in the devil.'

'What?'

'I believe in God, but I am also perfectly certain that the devil exists too—the anti-Christ, if you like. Oh not some hideous looking creature with horns and a tail, but something evil nevertheless—very evil.'

'And God is responsible for everything good, while we lay the blame for everything evil at the devil's door . . . is that right?'

'That's a rather simplistic statement, but more or less correct.'

'Well, if God is so strong, why does He lose the battle so often? Shouldn't good overcome evil if your religion is ever to succeed?'

'It will, when we have learned what we have to learn.'

'I don't understand that.'

'When enough people give their lives to God, then good will overcome all that is evil. It is men that start wars, not God.'

'Men with the devil in them?'

'Men . . . and women . . . who allow themselves to be led by evil forces.'

'I don't think that I'm an evil person, but I don't have faith.'

'I'm sure you aren't evil, Elizabeth. You work for the good of your fellow man. It's just that you won't accept that you are doing God's work—but you are, you know.'

'There must be something lacking in me, Hugh, but I simply cannot believe, not as you do. I don't understand how you can be so sure.'

'We must talk again. I'd like to help you.'

'You think I need help?'

'Yes. I think there's a conflict in your heart—a question to which you can find no answer. You have no peace of mind, Elizabeth.'

After that first discussion, Hugh and I met frequently, sometimes in the gardens, but more often in the library.

My mind was not changed but I began to feel less sure of my own opinions. Hugh was so earnest in his argument and I wanted to believe. My problem was that I could not decide whether I wanted to believe in God or Hugh Maloney.

We became good friends and, for the first time since David, I realized I was falling in love.

*   *   *

A cold hand holds Elizabeth's useless one. It is the vicar's.

'And how are you, my dear?' the man of God asks.

Elizabeth stares at him.

His eyes are smiling and his words are kind. She knows that she should not hate this well-meaning fool, but she does. He represents everything that she has lost. The vicar is glowing with confidence in his own beliefs. Elizabeth wants to tell him that it is he who has built his life on sand, but she can only gaze, like an obedient child, into that self-satisfied face.

He moves on to another of his captive

listeners. Elizabeth is relieved. She turns her eyes to the window once more.

'You'd like to stay here, wouldn't you, Elizabeth?' It is dear Jennifer. 'You enjoy looking out over the gardens—I can see that.'

Elizabeth's eyes try to say:

'Yes—you're right, I do like it here.'

Jennifer understands.

'I'll come back for you a bit later on then.'

Jennifer leaves Elizabeth to her thoughts. The breeze blows through the trees in the garden. They look agitated, disgruntled by the disturbance. They too wish to be left in peace.

Elizabeth returns to Hugh.

*   *   *

It was Christmas Eve, 1943. We had hung some paper chains in here and there was a small Christmas tree standing in this window with a fairy on top, that some of the nurses had made out of white gauze. A glorious fire roared up the chimney. Several of us had gathered for an evening of relaxation, along with a few of the more mobile patients. That special Christmas atmosphere, which we were determined to create, was brewing up beautifully, war or no war . . . faith or no faith.

I remember thinking back to childhood Christmases, to that miserable Christmas—the nativity—no, not that. Never think of that again. For a short time I dwelt on happier

126

years, but I did not allow such sentimentality to linger and cause me to become nostalgic. Hugh was coming to spend the evening with me and that was all I cared about.

We had declared our love to each other, but our relationship had not progressed past the stage of a warm friendship with the reassurance of a comfortable, hardly ever passionate, goodnight kiss to conclude every meeting. This suited us both at that time. Our commitment to our work and the uncertainty which surrounded us all during the war did not allow wedding plans to be a priority in our lives.

We were happy in the love and trust that we shared.

When Hugh entered the room that Christmas Eve, I felt like a young girl again. I wanted to run and kiss him sensuously, but my position of responsibility, along with my years, suppressed my girlish enthusiasm and I delivered a very proper kiss on the cheek and a sisterly hug.

'Hello, you old heathen,' Hugh joked. 'I see you don't mind sharing in this particular Christian festival!' He pointed to the glass of sherry in my hand.

'I told you,' I argued playfully, 'you haven't converted me yet, but give it time—you might convince me.'

'Oh I'll keep trying! I like a challenge. And this is a particularly enjoyable one.'

'Seriously though, Hugh,' I said quietly, 'I do feel different now. I think it's probably because I've found you—because I'm really happy again. It's difficult to believe in a loving God, when no one on this earth loves you.'

'Well, you never need feel like that again, darling,' he murmured, reaching into his pocket and retrieving a small, black box. 'Will you wear my engagement ring, Elizabeth?'

'Oh yes!' I replied, needing to give no thought to my answer.

I held out my hand and Hugh placed a simple, diamond solitaire on my finger.

'I should have waited until we were completely alone,' Hugh said, 'but we so seldom are. And Christmas Eve seemed such a good time to give you the ring.'

I glanced around the library at my assembled colleagues and patients.

'The presence of these people can't spoil this moment for us,' I whispered, 'nothing can, because we love each other.'

Hugh bowed his head and kissed me with a tenderness that caused my whole body to tingle.

'As soon as this war is over,' he said, 'we will marry. Let's pray that it won't be long now.'

'I'll pray,' I uttered. 'I promise . . . I'll pray.'

At these words, absolute delight spread over Hugh's placid face.

We embraced and kissed again. Now, no one else in the world, let alone the room, existed.

*   *   *

Soon after the rather subdued New Year celebrations, we were plunged into a spell of arctic-like weather. We had several weeks of hard frosts interspersed with quite heavy downfalls of snow.

I remember one night in particular. Hugh drove over from the camp to spend my off-duty evening with me. We had had an exceptionally tiring week on the wards, and I felt that I had to get away from starched uniforms and the smell of disinfectant. Hugh and I donned our heavy coats and boots, and walked out into the freezing cold night.

It was perfectly still outside. There was not the slightest breeze. A layer of snow had turned the garden into a white world, where the navy blue sky hung low and was awesome in its infinity. The biting frost had made the snow crisp on top and our feet made a wonderful crunching sound as we walked.

'Shall we build a snowman?' Hugh asked, hugging me closely to him.

'Don't be so childish! You'll be wanting a snowball fight next!'

'Well—why not?'

He picked up a handful of snow and pounded it into shape with his leather-gloved hands. Then he threw it towards the rose garden. It travelled through the silent darkness until it hit the brick wall with a soft thud and shattered into a fine, white powder.

'Men! You never grow up—not really!'

We laughed and Hugh kissed me with such fervent affection that the coldness was momentarily banished.

'What's behind that wall?' he inquired nonchalantly.

'I don't know, probably an old rose garden or something like that.'

I had not told a single soul that Maramar Grange was my old home. I think I was somehow ashamed of my wealthy beginnings, or perhaps I feared that my friends would behave differently towards me if they were aware of my true connections with this lovely old house. Of course, I knew that I would have to tell Hugh—when the right moment came.

'Let's go and have a look,' Hugh suggested, guiding me towards the entrance of the rose garden.

'No! No! I don't want to!' I shouted, stopping and pulling hard against his arm.

'All right,' he said, obviously startled by my adamant outburst. 'I wondered what was in there, that's all.'

'Yes,' I replied, calming myself, 'actually, I feel a bit tired, let's go back to the house, shall we?'

We walked back in silence.

That night, after Hugh had left, I was alone

in the library. The fire was dying in the grate, so I pulled a chair up close to make the most of its remaining warmth.

I had behaved foolishly in the garden and hoped that Hugh had thought no more about it. When he had suggested going into the rose garden, though, a kind of panic had gripped me. It was as though I could not allow Hugh to intrude. As much as I loved him, that rose garden was David's and mine and I did not want to share it with Hugh. It was such a precious part of my past. It seemed almost as if David was still there, in the rose garden. I felt that, if I had gone there with Hugh, I would have been betraying my first love.

For some time I gazed into the black and golden coals. I thought again of David and of our lost child, and what might have been, all those years ago.

Then I went to my room and thanked God for Hugh Maloney. My faith was returning to me.

*   *   *

Jennifer wheels Elizabeth back to her little cell.

'I'll take you to look out of that window another day, shall I, Elizabeth?' she suggests. 'It's a beautiful room, isn't it? And a lovely view over the gardens. Of course, I suppose it must have been a family home once, this old house. I wish I could turn the clock back so that I could see what it was like then.'

Elizabeth thinks that she would love to take Jennifer into the past with her, right into her memories and thoughts so that this caring young woman's wish might be granted.

Jennifer continues:

'They must have been wealthy—the people who lived here. Fancy having a huge mansion like this for your home—and servants and everything too! We can't imagine it, can we, Elizabeth?'

In her heart and in her mind, Elizabeth smiles.

*　　　*　　　*

At the end of February, Hugh and I found ourselves with a day off from our duties which happily we could share. It was so rare for our free days to coincide that we decided to go somewhere together to mark the occasion.

Brighton was settled upon.

We left early, in an old van that was kept at the camp for the use of the chaplain.

'Will this ancient contraption get us to Brighton?' I asked, as the vehicle's reluctance to start became obvious.

'Don't talk like that, she's sensitive,' Hugh explained, 'you'll hurt her feelings.'

He turned the starting handle again in desperation, whilst muttering a few less than

132

holy words under his breath. The engine's hesitant chugging and spluttering gained noisy momentum and, at last, we were off.

'We must be mad!' I observed, as we left Maramar Grange far behind us.

'Why?'

'Well look at us,' I replied, feigning bewildered astonishment at our actions. 'It's a cold, damp, February day and here we are making for the seaside in an old van that should have been scrapped years ago.'

'Mm—fun, isn't it?' Hugh cast a sideways glance at me and grinned.

'I just hope we don't break down!' I said.

We reached an extremely rain soaked Brighton at about half past ten and decided to look for a café of some sort in which to warm ourselves with the help of a hot drink. Everywhere along the sea front was, very sensibly, shut down for the winter. In the town, however, we found a friendly little teashop. Having parked the van nearby, we made a dash for the welcoming hospitality of the 'Willow Tea Rooms'.

Though the toast could have been hotter and the tea stronger, we felt better for nourishment. We sat staring out at the weather, debating what our next move should be.

'I think the rain's stopped,' Hugh said, with more hope than conviction in his voice.

'You're not going to suggest a walk along

133

the sea front, are you?' I asked tentatively.

'Of course! You can't come to Brighton without taking the sea air, Elizabeth! Come on, it'll get all that ether and stuff out of your lungs.'

'All right.' I gave in grudgingly. 'But I think I'd rather stick with the ether!'

It had just about stopped raining as we walked briskly along the promenade, taking deep breaths, at Hugh's insistence, in order to benefit fully from the invigorating sea air.

After a while, we sat down in one of those little three-sided hut affairs that one always finds in seaside towns, and stared out across the English Channel.

'Elizabeth,' Hugh began with almost boyish apprehension, as he held my hand. 'I've never asked you before, but that wedding ring you always wear—was it your mother's?'

'No . . . someone else's mother's.'

'I see.' Hugh touched the ring fondly. 'And he was very important to you, wasn't he?'

'How did you know it was a he?'

'I just did.'

'Yes—yes, he was very important to me, but he was killed in the First World War.'

'I thought it might be something like that.'

'Long ago and far away,' I whispered.

'Yes—I understand.'

Hugh did not question me about David. I never thought he would. He was far too sensitive—too kind.

He put his arm around me and I felt protected from all the old anguish—all the old pain. We gazed at the endless, bleak sea for ages, not speaking—not needing to.

'Shall we look for somewhere to have lunch?' I more suggested than asked, after quite some time. 'It's getting chilly now.'

'Good idea.'

We walked back along the promenade to a small hotel, which advertised meals for non-residents. The dining room was not spacious, but clean, and the food smelt tempting. Apart from two elderly gentlemen sitting at a nearby table, we were alone.

'Do you think this hotel is the sort of place that comedians joke about on the wireless?' I asked in all seriousness.

'Mm?'

'You know—Brighton—illicit meetings—Mr. and Mrs. Smith—and all that.'

'Meetings?'

Hugh was very involved with his meat pie and mash.

'Yes. Don't be obtuse—couples—dirty weekends—you know,' I whispered furtively.

'Oh!' Hugh laughed.

'You wretch!' I giggled. 'You knew what I meant all the time. You just enjoyed watching me trying to explain.'

'Yes, I did,' he admitted, still laughing. 'For someone who's been a nurse for so many years, you're a bit prim sometimes, Elizabeth.'

'Prim?'

'Oh, please don't take offence—it's delightfully refreshing in this day and age.'

'Mm, well, don't laugh at me—that's all.'

'Sorry—I won't.'

Hugh reached across the table and took my hand. His smiling eyes fixed on mine and joy quickly turned to mutual yearning.

'Talking of illicit meetings in small seaside hotels,' I whispered.

'What are you suggesting, Sister Purley?' Hugh asked, with false consternation and a teasing grin.

'I'm suggesting that we take a double room for the afternoon,' I replied.

'And I said that you were a bit prim!'

'Yes, you did, and it felt like a challenge.'

'Well it wasn't meant as one, I can assure you, Elizabeth.'

'Are you shocked and disgusted with me?'

'No—neither—I'm deeply in love with you.'

'I know.'

'Elizabeth . . .'

'Oh look, Hugh,' I interrupted, 'I know that you're a religious man, but we aren't a couple of children, are we? We both know our own minds and neither of us is married or anything like that.' I paused, amazed at my own boldness. 'Listen to me—just listen to me! I could never say such things to any other man on this earth but you—you're so special to me. I need you very much, Hugh.'

136

'And the fact that we aren't married doesn't worry you?'

'I know that it would do in normal circumstances, now that you've converted me back, at least some of the way, to Christianity. But with this awful war dragging on, I just feel that we should grab our happiness while we can. We can't be certain about tomorrow, can we?'

Hugh did not answer. Instead, he led me to the reception desk and booked a double room for Mr. and Mrs. Maloney. The young receptionist's expression remained impassive, as she handed Hugh the keys.

Our room had only one small window, which allowed in just enough light to reveal a brass bedstead, a slightly worn green eiderdown, a washstand, complete with chipped bowl and jug and, next to the door, a single wardrobe.

We both looked around us at this cheerless place.

'This is not what I had planned for us,' Hugh said, almost apologetically.

'But it isn't important,' I argued, looking up and finding an intensity in his eyes which I had never seen before.

We kissed. I was immersed in my need for him.

As we sank down on to the bed, Hugh nestled his face in my neck, but then, when his fingers reached for the buttons on my blouse, he snatched his hand away and stood up.

Standing with his back to me and his head bowed he sighed with agonizing resolve.

'No. Elizabeth,' he said, 'you're far too good for this. You deserve so much more.'

I went to him and massaged his shoulders with my fingertips.

'Hugh, I love you,' I murmured.

'Yes, and I love you.' He turned to face me and held my hands in his. 'And that's why we're getting out of this ghastly little room right now.'

He helped me on with my coat and we left the hotel, making straight for the van.

On the journey back to Maramar Grange we were both occupied with our own emotions—our own thoughts.

Had I been with anyone but Hugh, I would have felt cheapened by my behaviour at Brighton, but with him, I could never feel ashamed of my desires, or of the fact that I had let them be known to him.

Hugh made me feel like a woman, but a woman to be treated with respect, to be placed in a position of something close to worship in his heart.

I wondered if I would be able to live up to his high moral standards when we were married. I would try to—of that I was certain.

As we drove back, along the drive of this dear old house, Hugh stopped the van.

'We won't wait until the end of the war,

Elizabeth,' he said, touching my cheek. 'The way things are going, that could be a long way off. We'll marry soon—April or May—what do you think?'

'I think we'd better,' I replied. 'We'll start making the wedding arrangements tomorrow.'

That night, I fell asleep knowing that I was the happiest woman alive, and feeling unworthy of the man who would soon be my husband.

*   *   *

Hugh's protective restraint at that hotel in Brighton deepened my love for him so much that, when I was not with him, I felt incomplete and lost. His principles and sheer goodness made him perfect in my eyes.

I could trust this wonderful man of God.

*   *   *

It seemed, at that time, that nothing could spoil my second chance of real happiness. Hugh was not even fighting in the war; I could not lose him as I had lost David.

The wedding plans were underway. We were to be married in April.

A new light had entered my life . . . a light which I thought would endure.

*   *   *

A new day begins. Elizabeth's breakfast is brought in by Denise, her Welsh voice preceding her by a few seconds.

'Here we are, my lovely—scrambled eggs!' she warbles.

A noise—an unfamiliar noise alarms Elizabeth.

Denise reassures:

'Don't worry about that drilling, my lovely, we've got the builders in!'

Denise feeds Elizabeth.

The vulgar wailing of the drill and then the pounding of a hammer cause Elizabeth's head to ache. She wants to put her hands over her ears, but she cannot.

'It's something to do with some old pipes under the floors,' Denise goes on. 'They reckon it'll only take a couple of hours. I hope they're right. We can't put up with this row for long, can we?'

Elizabeth wants to go back to bed, but she is put into her wheelchair, cleaned and combed. Denise pushes her out on to the balcony. At least it is a little quieter out there.

*   *   *

It was early spring—March—when my life was once again shattered by an unexpected crisis.

I was supervising the cleaning of a particularly nasty infected stomach wound,

140

when a young nurse informed me that a Squadron Leader Hackett wanted to see me on a matter of some importance and urgency. My initial response was to send a message to him, stating that the work in which I was presently engaged was of the utmost importance, and that the Squadron Leader would have to wait until I had finished.

The idea that I should leave my duties and hurry to see an officer, who probably wanted to discuss some new memorandum sent by the War Office, which would have nothing to do with the healing of the wounded, made me angry. So, when I met the Squadron Leader, I was abrupt with him—unfairly so.

'This is a very busy time!' I declared, as I entered the library, where he was waiting for me. 'Is this visit really necessary, Squadron Leader? I am a nursing sister, you know, not a member of His Majesty's armed forces!'

'If you'll give me a minute to explain, Sister Purley, I think you'll understand why my meeting with you is extremely important.'

The officer's eyes were grave and anxiety swiftly replaced the impatience within me.

'What is it?' I asked.

'I believe you are engaged to the air force chaplain—Hugh Maloney,' he said solemnly.

'Why? What's happened to him?' I pleaded, grasping the arms of the chair into which I had sunk.

'Nothing—he's perfectly well.'

'What IS all this about then?' I snapped, my anger quickly returning, accompanied by enormous relief.

'You would say that you have a close relationship with Maloney?' the Squadron Leader went on, obviously ignoring my indignation.

'Yes, we're to be married next month, but I don't see that it has anything to do with you!'

'Does he talk to you about his work?'

'Not much—why?'

'Is he usually left alone with the airmen he sees here?'

'Well, yes. Faith is seen as a private matter in this hospital, Squadron Leader Hackett.'

'Very commendable.'

'What on earth are you getting at?'

'Have you noticed whether Maloney has spent more time with some of the men than with others?'

'I am far too busy to measure the duration of Hugh's visits. Anyway, I have no doubt that some of the men need more of a chaplain's time than others do.' I seethed at Hackett's arrogance. 'Now, I must refuse to answer any more of your questions until you tell me what this is all about!'

He stood up and walked to the fireplace, as though not wanting to face me while making his reply.

'We have reason to believe that Hugh Maloney is spying for Germany,' he said coldly.

'Don't be ridiculous!'

My voice and my face showed outrage, but in my heart I felt fear as well as disbelief.

'It's never easy to accept . . .'

'Accept!' I shouted. 'I don't accept! Hugh is a man of God—he would never betray his country!'

'He wouldn't be the first priest to turn traitor.'

'You accept that he's a priest then?'

'Oh yes, that's all been checked, of course. Hugh Maloney was ordained. We have no doubt that he is a priest.'

'Then how can you believe . . . ?'

'Sister Purley, I know that this must be devastating for you,' the Squadron Leader interrupted, showing a stony sympathy for the first time, 'but please . . . think for a moment. Who better for the men to confide in when they come home from the front, than a priest?'

'Yes, I see that, but . . .'

'Oh we're not too worried about the ranks. There's not much that those poor devils can give away. No, it's the officers he comes to see and particularly those with access to intelligence. We've been suspicious for some time.'

'Why?'

I was totally bewildered and refused to believe the allegations. Hugh was the most honest and upright of men.

'The enemy has had prior knowledge of our movements . . . our intentions if you like . . . on several occasions.'

'So?'

'So, in most instances, we have traced a link back to officers receiving treatment in this hospital. Officers who have talked to the trusted chaplain, believing their words to be in the strictest confidence, and needing to talk to someone about what they have seen . . . about what they know.'

'But it can't be Hugh!'

'We would not make such an accusation if we were not sure, Sister Purley.'

'How *can* you be sure? You said that you have reason to believe—what reason?'

'We set a trap. We told an officer, who was on his way here for treatment. of our suspicions concerning the chaplain. He agreed to help us. We gave him false information—position and movement of troops and armaments—all that sort of thing—and asked him to tell Maloney, and no one else, the bogus facts. This he did. Germany is now in possession of those facts. The chaplain is the only one who could have passed the information to the enemy.'

'No—I refuse to believe this! It must have been someone else! It can't have been Hugh! If you knew the man as I do, you would never make such ludicrous accusations!'

'I'm sorry, but it's the truth.'

Squadron Leader Hackett sat down next to me.

'I won't believe you! I'll never believe you!' I cried, unable to stop the tears.

'I came here because we wanted to make sure that you weren't involved—being his fiancée.'

'What?'

'It's all right. I'm satisfied that you were not aware of Maloney's actions. We won't be troubling you again.'

'What about Hugh? What will happen to him?'

'He'll be put under arrest. There's no other course open to us. Then he'll be court-martialled. I really am very sorry, Sister Purley. Goodbye now.'

The Squadron Leader left me more alone than I had been for many years. In my heart was fear, in my mind, torment. My world was darkening.

*　　　*　　　*

Though I absolutely refused to believe that Hugh was guilty of this most dreadful of crimes, I was also aware that I would be unable to persuade his seniors of his innocence.

Total panic surged through me. How could I help him?

I rushed from the room, not knowing where

145

I was going or why, but realizing that to stand dithering in the library was a waste of precious time.

To my amazement, Hugh was coming down the stairs.

'You're here already!' I called inanely.

'Yes,' Hugh replied, that familiar smile belying everything that I had just been told about him, and reinforcing my views on the stupidity of the allegations. 'I know I'm early, but it was such a glorious morning that I decided to walk across the fields and get an early start. I've only got two more men to see.'

I grabbed his arm and pulled him into the library as though it were some kind of sanctuary.

'Listen to me, Hugh,' I whispered.

'What's wrong, Elizabeth?'

'Squadron Leader Hackett has just been here.'

'Hackett?'

'Yes—he's working with R.A.F. intelligence—and—and he tried to convince me that you . . .'

'Sister Purley—come quickly—Sister!'

A young nurse barged into the room, her face grave and anxious.

'What is it?' I snapped.

'Haemorrhage! Young Cookson—please come!'

I had no choice.

'Wait here!' I called to Hugh as I hurried

from the room.

It took a good half an hour to deal with the emergency. I remember that Cookson survived—that was, however, sparse consolation.

When I returned to the library, my apron still splattered with the young man's blood, the sight that met my eyes filled me with such horror that I almost lost consciousness.

In the middle of the library ceiling a large hook still remained. When I was a girl, it had supported the chandelier. Hugh had taken one of the cords which held back the heavy curtains, threaded it through the hook and hung himself. His face was distorted and blue. His body, like a carcass of beef in a slaughterhouse, was suspended there—dead, but without dignity.

I stared, with eyes which could not cry, at the scene before me. The room was in disarray. Some of my colleagues were clambering up to Hugh. I did not know why. He was beyond all help.

I cannot remember the rest of that day with any clarity. It was a nebulous tunnel of despair.

*　　*　　*

Elizabeth is tired.

She can hear the workmen inside the house. They are attacking her old home.

Today's memories are intolerably painful,

yet it is as if she is driven to relive them. Surely, though, this is the end of her search.

This must be her answer.

*   *   *

I did not attend Hugh's funeral. At the time he was due to be buried, I went to the spinney and put his engagement ring into a jackdaw's nest. I remember hoping that one of the birds I had watched from my window might carry it to someone who needed money.

I wanted to keep nothing of Hugh's. It was not that I had stopped loving him—quite the reverse. My sense of loss was so great that the only way I could cope was to try and obliterate him from my mind. A strange way to grieve, no doubt, but it was my way. Not only had I lost the man I loved, but also that most special of gifts that he had given back to me—my faith.

He had seemed like the definitive Christian, someone on whom I would always be able to depend. His so-called belief in God had appeared so alive and strong that I had accepted it as real. This man, whom I had thought to be so righteous, was a traitor. When I had believed him to be bringing comfort to the wounded and dying, he had been eliciting information to feed to the enemy.

Had he been innocent, he would never have taken his own life; he would have fought to clear his name. I was sure of that . . . as sure as

I could be of anything.

I had fallen in love with the most despicable of men and, though I could not hate him, I hated myself for doing so. I found myself despising the faith he had professed to uphold.

Once again the foundations of my life had fallen away from me. Once more, I was forsaken and wretched.

*   *   *

Elizabeth is pushed back into the house.

She feels a tiredness which seems simply too heavy to overcome.

'I'll put you on your bed for a while,' Jennifer says. 'You look tired.'

A blanket is draped over Elizabeth's legs.

The workmen have stopped hammering and drilling. There could be peace . . . but . . . there is something else. It is in this house . . . Elizabeth knows there is something.

'Hey look, Jennifer!' Denise rushes into the room. 'Oh, sorry, lovely—all right are you?' The Welsh one goes up to Jennifer and whispers. 'Look, look at what one of the workmen just found!'

'What?'

'It's a letter. It was under the floor in the old library. It must have slipped down behind the skirting board or through the floorboards or something. It's really old. It had never been opened.'

149

'Well, look at that!'

'I wonder who wrote it . . .' Denise reads aloud.

'My darling Elizabeth . . .'

Elizabeth opens her eyes wide. She listens, with wonder, to Jennifer and Denise.

'It must be a love letter,' Jennifer says. 'It doesn't seem right to read it . . . it's private.'

Elizabeth wills Denise to read the letter; if only she could take it and read it herself.

'Oh, they'll all be dead by now. Look, it says, March 1944.' Denise is determined. 'What does it matter? Listen!

'My darling Elizabeth,
I do not know if I can express what I feel by writing a letter but I must try. I have to take my own life, my dear, because I cannot face being called a traitor in the eyes of the law— man's law remember—not God's. Yes, Elizabeth, I am a priest and a Christian— truly.

You see, I believe that all war is wrong and against the will of God. It is immaterial to me who wins—England or Germany. We are all God's children, after all. Surely a genuine Christian cannot despise a whole nation. I feel no hatred at all for the so-called enemy—I feel no hatred for anyone.

The only aim in my heart has been to end the carnage and to restore peace. I was convinced, at the beginning, that Germany would be the victor. So, I decided to speed up the whole horrifring business by helping them to win as quickly as possible. You see, I have always thought of myself as a human being rather than an Englishman.

I believed that I was doing God's will. I have always believed that. Please try to understand and forgive.

I love you, Elizabeth. Pray for me and always keep your faith.

Hugh'

A tear runs down Elizabeth's cheek. Her heart is full of love and her mind finds true contentment.

She knows now that her dear Hugh had not been an evil man, but a true Christian—albeit a misguided one. He had acted as he did only because of his love for his fellow man, and his longing for the return of peace to the world. Because she knows this, Elizabeth can have faith once more.

'I'm going to show the others!' Denise exclaims, hurrying from the room.

'Are you all right, Elizabeth?' Jennifer asks kindly, as she sits down on the bed and takes Elizabeth's hands.

Everywhere seems quiet. The world is in twilight.

Hugh's letter has reached her and Elizabeth has found her answer. She closes her eyes and says a silent prayer to a God in whom she can

151

trust at last. To the God who brought her home, so that she would know the truth.

There are no weeping relatives around Elizabeth's bed as she takes her last breath.

There is no more light . . . not in this world.

* * *

Elizabeth is dead.

* * *

'Hello, my name is Edward Carlin,' announces a man of about thirty years old, in a loud Australian voice.

He seems to fill the reception area in the lobby of the old people's home.

'Oh, and what can I do for you?' chirps the Welsh one, charmed by this suntanned vision of masculinity.

'Well,' Mr. Carlin begins, 'I've lived in Perth all my life, you see—Australia—you probably noticed the accent, Miss . . . ?'

'Miss Evans,' Denise replies with a coquettish turn of the head. 'Oh yes, I noticed the accent.'

'Well, to cut a long story short, Miss Evans, my father was adopted by a young English couple—the Carlins—when he was only a few days old.'

Denise nods and utters a bewildered,
'Mm?'

'And they took him to Australia where he's lived all his life—still going strong, in fact.'

'Oh good,' the Welsh one says apprehensively.

'Yeah, well when the old man told me about the adoption and everything, I got a bit curious. I guess I'm just one of those people who needs to know about his ancestors—his true roots—you know?'

'I see . . . yes . . .'

'Well, Dad was able to give me quite a lot of information because the Carlins had told him about his natural parents before they died. Good of them, wasn't it?'

'Oh, yes—very good.' Denise nods, almost frantically.

'It turns out that my real grandfather was a man called Edward—I guess I was named after him—Edward Purley, and my grandmother was a Miss Isobel Treherne.'

'Oh,' the Welsh one puts in, with some understanding of the situation beginning to emerge in her less than brilliant mind.

'Now, apparently my real grandparents have both passed away. I've been through all kinds of birth certificates and documents! You wouldn't believe it!'

'No, I can imagine,' Denise sympathizes.

'Anyway, the upshot is, that Edward Purley had one sister called Elizabeth. She never married apparently, but I've traced her to this place.'

153

'Yes, I see . . . but . . .'

'Now she is, as far as I can find out, my only living relative, and I'd dearly like to talk to her.'

'But . . .'

Denise raises a hand as a signal that she has something of importance to say, but the enthusiastic Australian will not be halted.

'You see, these Purleys were apparently quite a wealthy family, not that that's all I'm interested in—no, not at all. I'd just love to meet the old lady and find out what I can from her about my real family.'

'Mr. Carlin,' the Welsh one says, her voice now charged with urgency. 'I'm afraid that you're about half an hour too late.'

'What?'

'There's no other way to break it to you. Miss Elizabeth Purley passed away about thirty minutes ago.'

'Oh hell—no!' Mr. Carlin is clearly astounded by his bad luck. 'Thirty minutes!' he echoes. 'Oh hell!'

'She was one hundred years old,' Denise explains, 'and she wouldn't have been able to answer your questions, I'm afraid. She had a stroke a while back and she never recovered her speech. She was almost totally paralyzed too.'

'Poor old soul.'

'Yes, she had no quality of life in the end. You mustn't feel too sorry that she's gone. For

154

her, it's probably the best thing.'

'I could have visited her though . . . told her who I was . . . I could have talked to her.'

'It wouldn't have done any good, Mr. Carlin,' the Welsh one sings. 'She wouldn't have understood. You see, her mind was completely gone.'